THE CASE OF THE
PECULIAR INHERITANCE

A

MYSTERY NOVEL

SAMANTHA ST. CLAIRE

Copyright © 2021 by Samantha St. Claire

All rights reserved. Thank you for supporting the continued work of authors and publishers by buying an authorized edition of this book and for complying with copyright laws by not reproducing, scanning, storing, downloading, reverse engineering, or distributing any part of this work in any form without permission. The publisher and author do not control and do not assume any responsibility for third-party websites or their content. For permission requests, write to the publisher, via the contact page on the website below. For information about special discounts available for bulk purchases and sales promotions, contact the publisher at books@cambronpublishing.com.

Published by Trappers Peak Publishing
Bigfork, Montana 59911
www.trapperspeakpublishing.com
www.cambronpublishing.com

Publisher's Note: This is a work of fiction. Names, characters, places, and incidents are a product of the author's imagination or are used fictitiously. Locales and public names are sometimes used for fictitious and atmospheric purposes. Any resemblance to actual people, living or dead, or to businesses, companies, events, institutions, or locales is entirely coincidental.

The Case of the Peculiar Inheritance; novel/Samantha St. Claire
ISBN: 978-1734864014

Cover Design by MK McClintock
Cover Background © TeriVirbickis | Deposit Photos
Woman in Dress | Shutterstock

PRAISE FOR THE WRITINGS OF
SAMANTHA ST. CLAIRE

"A wonderful book, and an auspicious start to The Sawtooth Range series!" —*InD'Tale Magazine* on *Kat's Law*

". . . a surprise ending which will delight fans of romance/adventure novels who have read too many scripted endings. This is a terrific read, a great novel!" —*Readers Favorite*

"Reading this wonderful book, *Comes the Winter*, is like finding yourself in your favorite chair, near a crackling fire, when it's cold outside. Weather is changeable and so is life, but you are in a warm and happy place." —*The Constant Reader*

"...a beautiful, poignant and captivating work of fiction." —*Readers' Favorite* on *A Portrait of Dawn*

"Samantha St. Claire delivers a well-researched historical romance mystery that had me smiling through tears as I turned the last page. The characters are likable and full of depth, and I thoroughly enjoyed the vivid descriptions of the terrain, era, and the overall canvas of the story. My favorite character, Maddie, is fiery, intelligent, honorable, and ready to handle anything that comes her way. A true survivor. I highly recommend *Redeeming Lies* to anyone who enjoys a smart, romantic read." —*Readers' Favorite*

THE SAWTOOTH RANGE SERIES
Kat's Law
High Valley Promise
Comes the Winter
Redeeming Lies
A Portrait of Dawn
A Hartmann Ranch Christmas

McKENZIE SISTERS MYSTERY SERIES
The Case of the Peculiar Inheritance

WHITCOMB SPRINGS SERIES
"Healing Fire"
"Tracking Amy"
"The Unwitting Hero of Whitcomb Springs"
"Harvest Promise"

Samantha St. Claire also writing as Jan Karol Tanaka
Misha Alexandrov

For those friends who teach us
to be strong and courageous.

CHAPTER 1

Denver, Colorado 1899

The explosion was small compared to her previous miscalculations, blowing out only one window of the study and merely scorching the hem of the damask drapes covering it. Miss Rose McKenzie and her housekeeper, Mrs. Constance Pennyworth, quickly extinguished the subsequent fire. The housekeeper tore down the damaged drapes and threw them on the remnants of Rose's ruined experiment.

After she raised the window sashes to give the cloud of acrid smoke somewhere to go besides their lungs, she collapsed on the stool across from Rose. The housekeeper fanned her face with her soot-covered apron and grumbled, "Well now, what have you learned from that experiment, Miss Rose? I surely hope it was worth the expense of a broken window and two rather costly drapes."

Rose pulled a pencil from the mass of auburn curls pinned high on her head and scribbled notes on the still-smoking clipboard. "Reduce the potassium chloride to magnesium ratio."

Mrs. Pennyworth pushed herself to her feet with a small grunt and heaved a sigh of surprising force for a woman so small in stature. "I came upstairs to ask if you wanted me to bring your breakfast up. If you recall, you didn't eat your supper last night."

Rose tapped the pencil against the clipboard and surveyed the disheveled state of the laboratory. "I suppose I should eat downstairs this morning." Mrs. Pennyworth's scowl transformed into an expression of concern.

She rounded the table with impressive speed for a woman who'd seen more than a half-century of birthdays come and go. She grasped Rose's face in her two calloused hands and leaned in for closer inspection. "Why, you're bleeding!" This time she expressed her opinion with a disapproving cluck of her tongue. "Miss Rose, you are going to do yourself in one day with all this experimenting." She blew another ponderous breath. "I'm going to ring Dr. Whitman. That might need stitches."

Rose drew the back of her hand to dab at her temple, surprised to feel the sticky evidence of Mrs. Pennyworth's pronouncement. "Hmm. I would have expected more blood from a head wound." She rose quickly from her stool and stepped to the wall mirror, inspecting her forehead with sharp interest. "It's a clean cut. It might even develop into a quite colorful bruise. You're right, Mrs. Pennyworth, I should probably have it tended to." Rose shook small shards of glass from her lab apron and observed brightly, "I've never had stitches. I'm most interested in the experience."

As her housekeeper stormed off, the exasperated blow from

her lips sent a good portion of smoke out the open windows. "I'll give the doctor a call and set another place for breakfast."

"Oh, did I forget to tell you? We're going to the museum today. There's an exhibit on the embalming techniques of Egyptian mummies, which promises to be interesting."

"I approve of your company, but to my way of thinking, you've a morbid fascination with death." Mrs. Pennyworth harrumphed as she left the room, her footsteps hammering down the staircase.

"THAT SHOULD DO IT." Dr. Taylor Whitman sat back and studied Rose with amber eyes that reminded her of brandy in candlelight. At the moment, his eyes had a wolfish glint as he perused her with something more than clinical interest. The moment passed quickly, and the softness returned as his lips curved into a wide smile, revealing normal teeth with no pronounced canines. Except for the thin diagonal scar creasing his right eyebrow, he was a decidedly perfect specimen of manhood. Not for the first time, Rose wondered how a man of such bearing should have wielded a scalpel instead of a sword.

The doctor reached out and touched the tip of her nose. "You're a very lucky young woman, Miss McKenzie. If that piece of metal had struck you an inch lower, you could have lost the use of that attractive blue eye."

Rose touched her temple, fingering the stitches. "Only two?"

Dr. Whitman shook his head. "You have my deepest

sympathies, Mrs. Pennyworth. I think the patient has not only a laceration but a brain injury as well."

"Is that what you call it? A brain injury? If it is, I think she had it before the explosion." Mrs. Pennyworth huffed and left the room, calling back, "If you've an interest, there's breakfast chilling in the morning room."

With less humor in his eyes, the doctor turned back to Rose, his smooth brow creased in disapproval. "Seriously, Rose, you need to be more careful. You push your studies too far sometimes. Magnesium is unstable in the best of situations. Do you know how many photographers have been maimed and even killed by mishandling it?"

Rose met his intense gaze with her own studious one.

The doctor frowned. "Did you hear me?"

"Did you know that your left eye has gold radial lines? It's only in the left eye. Like striations one might find in gold ore. Fascinating," she said as she shifted her focus from one eye to the other. "One day you must tell me how you came by that scar." She touched her fingertip to his warm skin and traced the thin line stretching from his hairline to his eyebrow.

Dr. Whitman brushed her hand aside. "You're impossible."

"And you're angry."

With lips compressed and frustration apparent, he snapped his medical bag closed. For a long moment, he stared at her before shaking his head and taking a step to the door.

Rose reached for his wrist and gripped it firmly. "No, I can tell. You're angry. Your right eye twitches, like now. You can feel it, can't you? There! I saw it again. I wonder if it's in rhythm with your pulse. Have you ever tried timing it?"

Dr. Whitman gently but firmly plucked her hand from his sleeve. "Let's go to the museum, shall we? I believe we were going to try to arrive before the midday crowds."

"You're right! What time is it?" Rose started for the hallway. "I'll just pick up a wrap from my room."

"Miss McKenzie?" Mrs. Pennyworth rounded the corner, nearly colliding with her employer. "Excuse me." She stammered, bringing a hand to her breast. "There's a lady here to see you." The housekeeper looked over her shoulder, then leaned forward and whispered, "I think it's a professional visit. She asked for the dee-tec-tive." Mrs. Pennyworth always said the word in clearly distinguished syllables, making it sound like three separate words, and not very polite ones at that.

"Oh? Well, that's wonderful! Please, show her in."

"Perhaps I should leave you to speak with your client in private," Dr. Whitman said, already starting for the door.

"Oh, no! If she's distressed by some criminal activity, I'm quite certain your presence would comfort her. It's necessary for a client to feel relaxed in order to recall all the details of a case."

"If you think so." Dr. Whitman set his bag on the table and took a step back, folding his arms across his chest.

She nodded approvingly. "That's good. You look very professional standing just that way. How do I look?" She poked her fingers ineffectively into the precarious mass of curls atop her head. "I imagine my stitches give an impression of an adventurous nature. Do you agree?"

"Or that you are extremely clumsy." He grinned. "Or careless."

Mrs. Pennyworth prevented Rose from responding, but Rose shot him a narrow-eyed look.

"Mrs. Violet VanderHem, this is—" Mrs. Pennyworth began.

"Verbena," the woman corrected quickly. "It's Verbena Vander*Helm*, not Vander*Hem*."

Mrs. Pennyworth stiffened. "They're both flowers. Simple mistake. Miss McKenzie, this is Mrs. Vander*Helm*. She's here to seek your professional assistance." Mrs. Pennyworth stepped aside to allow the matronly woman to enter. However, before their visitor could take another step, a well-nourished Basset Hound pushed past her heavy skirts to make his way into the sitting room.

"Oh no you don't!" Mrs. Pennyworth stumbled forward and grabbed for the dog. "Sergeant, you naughty rascal! Come back here!"

The dog eluded her and took shelter behind Rose's skirt, before rolling a rebellious eye in the housekeeper's direction.

"It's all right, Mrs. Pennyworth. Sergeant can stay," Rose said sweetly.

Mrs. Pennyworth frowned her disapproval at the two of them. "As you wish, Miss." She smoothed her apron and left the room, muttering to herself.

Rose called after her, "Would you please bring a pot of tea?" Rose then stretched out her arm. "Mrs. VanderHelm, welcome. Won't you please be seated?"

THE CASE OF THE PECULIAR INHERITANCE

The woman crossed the room, while keenly observing the furnishings. "You possess an impressive home, Miss McKenzie. A Queen Anne, isn't it? It reminds me of one of Mr. Lang's designs, like the Brighton House on Downing Street. Such a marvelous variety of charming windows. Wasn't this home built by the Fitzhugh family?" With an expression of utmost curiosity, Mrs. VanderHelm sat silent for a moment before stating, "I don't believe you and I have met. It seems we should have. Is your father a trustee of the railroad?"

"No. He's deceased."

The woman remained standing as though expecting Rose to elaborate, which she did not. After an awkward moment of glancing to the handsome stranger at the back of the room and the noncommunicative Miss McKenzie, Mrs. VanderHelm took the proffered seat by the window.

Only then did Rose turn to introduce the doctor. "This is my friend, Dr. Whitman. He often assists me as a consultant on cases involving physical assaults or murder. You can speak freely before him."

Mrs. VanderHelm's eyes widened. "Heavens! I did not know women were engaged in such ghastly professions. You must be quite . . . strong of stomach."

"It helps, I suppose."

The older woman shifted her attention to the doctor, her expression brightening with something more than maternal interest. "Dr. Whitman, yes, didn't I read about you in the paper last month? A police investigation, I recall. The murder of that unfortunate bank president."

"Mr. Robert Thornbottom," Rose volunteered, pleased that the case had come to the woman's attention. It had been a most intriguing investigation, and more enjoyable due to its lethal component.

Mrs. VanderHelm continued to keep her eyes on the attractive doctor. "You identified the wife as the murderess. Poison, I believe. How ghastly!"

Dr. Whitman cleared his throat. "Actually, it was the investigative talents of Miss McKenzie that uncovered the wife's use of the digitalis plant to poison his tea over a period of several weeks." He inclined his head to Rose as he added, "Not even the police considered the possibility of murder. I simply confirmed Miss McKenzie's conclusions."

"Horrid business! It's good to know your medical knowledge is useful for solving our city's shameful crime problem."

Dr. Whitman frowned and tried again, "It was Miss—"

"Perhaps you knew my husband, Dr. William VanderHelm? Brilliant surgeon at St. Joseph Hospital."

Dr. Whitman shook his head. "I'm sorry. The name is unfamiliar to me, but I've only practiced here in Denver for the past two years."

"Oh, I see. That explains it, then. Dr. VanderHelm passed six years ago and would have undoubtedly been familiar to you if you had been living here."

Rose knotted her fingers in the folds of her skirt. Introductions could be such tiresome formalities. She recognized an opening in the dialog and prompted the woman to introduce the reason for her visit. "How may I be of help, Mrs. VanderHelm?"

Rose watched as the woman's expression shifted to one of dubious confidence.

"I have nowhere else to turn."

Rose stifled the sigh that welled in her throat. Most of her clients' introductions began in this manner with nearly the same phrasing. One day her reputation would repudiate such doubts of her abilities. Until then, she would need to build that reputation one case at a time. With a cheerful voice, she responded, "Well, I'm glad you found me." Recalling Dr. Whitman's recent suggestion to smile at her clients, she made an honest effort, but judging from the doctor's grimace, she assumed she'd failed in her attempt.

Mrs. VanderHelm commenced her story. "I tried the police. They did not think the theft a crime significant enough to warrant the use of their workforce. Imagine that! A founding citizen's home broken into and that violation is not sufficient cause for an investigation? They could have murdered me in my bed!"

Dr. Whitman moved behind Rose's chair, drawing Mrs. VanderHelm's eyes with him. He observed, "I'm certain that Miss McKenzie, being a woman, can appreciate your concern for safety and your need to be taken seriously. I'm sure the discovery was disturbing. This occurred last night?"

"Yes!"

"If you don't mind my interruption, before you tell the totality of your story, I'm certain Miss McKenzie would be interested to know how you heard of her services. Isn't that correct, Miss McKenzie?"

Rose felt the doctor's prodding finger between her shoulder blades. A moment passed as she worked out what appeared a coded message in his eyes. His left eyebrow arched at an acute angle, prompting Rose to turn her attention back to her client. "Yes. May I ask who referred you?"

"It was a young officer, unusually curly hair. An Irishman, I believe. Donahue. Yes, Detective Donahue." She pulled one of Rose's business cards from her handbag. "He gave me this."

Dr. Whitman leaned down close to Rose's ear. "A calling card," he whispered. "A waste of money, I believe you said."

This marketing was a constant source of irritation between them, with the doctor haranguing her about the need to advertise her services. Rose drilled him with a look of annoyance before addressing her client again. "About your case, Mrs. VanderHelm."

The dog lifted its head, giving a low "woof" as Mrs. Pennyworth reentered the room carrying a silver tea service. "Here you are. A fresh pot of Earl Grey," she said as she lowered the tray to the side table. "Shall I pour?"

"Mrs. VanderHelm, about the break-in."

Mrs. VanderHelm gave a nod to the housekeeper. "Yes, thank you. Two spoons of sugar, if you please."

Rose tapped her foot impatiently as Mrs. Pennyworth moved like a woman afflicted with advanced rheumatism. What had come over her?

THE CASE OF THE PECULIAR INHERITANCE

"Here you are, Mrs. Vander*Helm*. As they say, sweets for the sweet." She delivered the china cup into the woman's hand with a syrupy smile. Turning back to the tea tray, she offered to pour a cup for Dr. Whitman.

"Yes, please. No sugar."

The housekeeper poured the tea as though it was liquid gold, requiring the precision of an alchemist.

Dr. Whitman accepted the proffered cup with a charming smile. "Thank you."

"Miss McKenzie? Any tea for you?"

"No!"

Dr. Whitman's cup rattled in its saucer.

Rose winced, quickly adding, "No, thank you, Mrs. Pennyworth. That will be all we require for now."

Mrs. VanderHelm peered at Rose over the violet adorned teacup. Rose recalled the recent addition of stitches at her temple. She lifted her fingers to touch the tender skin and explained. "I suppose you're wondering about my injury."

"Um, no. Actually... Your hair. It's a rather remarkable shade of red, isn't it?"

Rose redirected her hand to brush a lock of hair back from her brow. "Copper," she corrected.

"I've noticed those with such hair as red as yours exhibit similarly colorful temperaments." The woman gave a tinkling laugh.

Dr. Whitman made a choking sound, and his cup clattered onto its saucer a second time.

"You may be correct in that assessment when one considers the famous historical personages that share the trait, George Washington and Thomas Jefferson just to name two." Rose gripped the arms of her chair and stood a little apart from Dr. Whitman, with whom she refused eye contact.

Rose redirected the drift of conversation back to the case. "You say the police found no reason to investigate this break-in. Why do you think that might be?"

"Because they stole nothing of value."

Her interest awakened, Rose crossed the room and sat in the chair closer to her client. "Please, go on."

"These hooligans broke my heirloom china and made a general mess of the kitchen and parlor, but that was the extent of the damage. I had priceless paintings, even jewelry hidden in my husband's study downstairs. They disturbed none of that."

"Was there a forced entry?" Rose asked.

"No! Shocking, isn't it?" Mrs. VanderHelm said, appearing more excited than disturbed that the criminal, as she referred to him, was possibly living under her roof.

Rose glanced over at the doctor, who had taken a seat in the chair she'd vacated. "Did they suggest that one of your household was the perpetrator?"

The woman looked offended and said tersely, "If by perpetrator, you mean thief?" The woman's thin nose expanded as her nostrils flared dangerously. "My staff comprises loyal women in whom I have unassailable faith."

"I see." Rose knew the probability for such loyalties to dissolve where financial gain was a possibility. Despite the woman's convictions, her staff would necessitate further investigation as chief suspects, having both the likelihood of motive and means. But if they stole nothing of value, then why?

"There's more I haven't told you." Mrs. VanderHelm whispered the next revelation as she reached into her handbag for the second time, withdrawing a large envelope and passing it into Rose's hand. "Three days ago, I received this from an attorney here in Denver, a Mr. Charles Kent. He's quite reputable. In fact, he's assisted me occasionally with finances related to my charitable work. You may know him?"

Rose shook her head as Dr. Whitman replied in kind.

Mrs. VanderHelm nodded at the evidence she'd given Rose. "Go ahead. You may open it."

Rose pulled the folded paper from the envelope, scanned the letter, and waited for the woman to continue her narrative.

"You see what it says? We have sent a gift from the estate of Mr. Raymond Larson. Just that and little more other than the firm's regrets concerning the passing of this Mr. Larson."

Rose surmised the police had rejected the case for good reason. "May I assume you knew Mr. Larson?" she asked, her interest cooling more rapidly than the tea in Mrs. VanderHelm's cup.

Mrs. VanderHelm sat back with a suggestion of a smile mingled with a peculiar expression of satisfaction. "No, you may not."

Rose frowned down at the letter, then lifted her eyes to the woman for explanation.

"You see? That's where the mystery begins. I *don't* know the man."

"You mean you don't recall meeting him?" Rose asked, suspecting for the first time that the woman might be more in need of the doctor's services than her own.

Mrs. VanderHelm wore her displeasure like a secondhand hat, ill-used and unflattering. "I said, I've never met the man. I am known for my remarkable memory of faces and names. It's a skill that has served me well in society. I rather think such a skill as I possess would be useful to someone in your line of work."

"Yes, I'm sure." Rose dismissed the comment and suppressed her irritation. "So, you received a gift from someone you don't know and have never met. What was the gift?"

The woman's smile broadened, pushing the wrinkles into a bunch before each ear. "Something of absolutely no value." She paused and savored the dramatic recounting of her story. "It was a vase of hideous design and color. I scarcely think it cost the man more than a few dollars. I would know these things, as I collect fine china."

"How is this connected to the break-in?" Rose asked, with bristling impatience.

Mrs. VanderHelm's left eyebrow rose to meet with a stiff curl on her brow, as her voice lowered to deliver an answer. "It's the one item the criminals took from my home—that one completely worthless vase."

CHAPTER 2

The VanderHelm house dominated the intersection of two major avenues, a sprawling brick edifice with more attention paid to square footage than elegance or charm. But the warm manner in which Mrs. VanderHelm received Rose and Dr. Whitman made up for the cold exterior.

At the back of the house, Rose knelt outside the exterior door to the kitchen, a magnifying glass in her hand. Dr. Whitman rocked on his heels with his hands thrust deep in his pockets. "Just why am I here?" he asked with no attempt to conceal his festering irritation.

"You have a means of expedient transportation." She lowered the glass. "I thought we had an appointment to visit the Egyptian exhibit this morning."

"Precisely. Here we are—*not* at the museum," he said.

"You're displeased."

Dr. Whitman gave out a stiff snort. "I'm here because you find my horse and buggy a better mode of travel than your normal mode of transportation, a bicycle. Why should I be displeased?"

"Good. It makes me anxious when you're displeased." Rose

resumed her examination of the lock through the magnifying glass for several more minutes. At last, she gave a triumphant, "Hah!" followed by, "Just as I

suspected. See here? Clear evidence on the lock of forced entry."

"You know that how?" Dr. Whitman asked. "When the police investigated and found nothing to suggest it, I am forced to inquire."

"If you doubt my findings, look here." She scooted to the side and passed the pearl-handled glass to the doctor.

The doctor glanced down at the dirt covering the steps, then at his neatly pressed trousers, shrugged, and kneeled beside her.

"See those lateral lines? There and there." She pointed out the grooves with a forefinger.

He lowered the glass and asked, "How do you know those aren't just the marks left by a key or someone fumbling with the lock? Not with a lock pick but with a key."

Rose smiled indulgently and shook her head. "Look again."

After delivering her a dubious expression, he complied, asking, "What am I looking for?"

"Close-set, parallel lines."

The doctor leaned closer, frowning as he squinted against the morning light reflecting off the polished brass. "Hmm. I see several patterns of parallel lines." He lowered the glass. "What does that prove?"

"It proves that the perpetrator was probably a professional who had experience picking locks." Rose held out a hand to the doctor, who shook his head and rose to stand beside her. "You don't believe me," she said.

The doctor flicked dust from his pants. "I didn't say that."

"You don't have to. I can see in your expression that you don't and that you find a lack of credulity in my summation."

"In truth, I'm having difficulty believing that you could determine someone picked this lock when the police did not."

"Dr. Whitman, how many cases have you seen me work upon where I found key elements overlooked by our police force?"

He sighed and nodded, a smile slowly creasing the corners of his eyes. "A few."

"I can put your doubts to rest. Let me show you what they used." Rose pulled a smaller cloth pouch from her leather investigation. Once opened, it revealed several small metal tools, no longer than five inches. She lifted one up between them, pointing to the straight-edged tip. "A lock pick, Dr. Whitman."

"Where in heaven's name did you acquire a set of lock picks?"

Rose shook her head, surprised that the intelligent doctor should ask such a question. "Tools of the criminal's trade should be among my own as an investigator. Don't you agree?"

His frown deepened. Before he could ask his initial question a second time, she extracted from her pocket a skeleton key. "This is the key to the lock. Do you see the parallel design of the tip? Those lines result from regular use of a key. But when you look closer, you can distinguish the deeper gouges made by one of these tools. The deeper lines are the ones more recently made."

He bent at the waist and peered at the lock again through the glass. "Yes, I can see them now."

"Do you want me to demonstrate?" Before he could answer, she used the skeleton key to lock the door. A moment of consideration passed before she selected one pick. She knelt before the door again and inserted the pick. Five minutes later, a quiet click and Rose turned the handle and pushed open the door.

Dr. Whitman applauded. "Yes, you convinced me. Impressive, as usual, Miss McKenzie. I should have learned by now not to doubt you."

Her triumph might have been complete had entry not taken five minutes. She blew out a quick puff of displeasure. "It appears that I need to perfect my skill in this area. Much too slow."

The doctor watched her return the pick to the pouch with the others and asked, "You still haven't told me how you came by these tools."

"I have my sources; besides, it would be unprofessional of me to divulge confidential information."

"MRS. EDNA HAYCRAFT." Mrs. VanderHelm's housekeeper drew out the syllables of her name, then winked at Rose and added, "It's a craft to grow good hay."

Rose lifted her pencil from the casebook where she'd been taking notes. The woman sitting across from her gave a chortle that fell just short of a laugh. She seemed to wait for some response from Rose. An extended moment passed with the women staring at each other, both equally baffled by the other.

"It's so you remember how to spell the name, you see?" The housekeeper offered the additional information followed by a quick, expectant smile.

Rose tapped her pencil against the notebook. "That's not logical. Hay production is agronomy not a craft. Blacksmithing, perhaps, or furniture construction. I think it would be difficult to make an argument for any aspect of farming." She brought the pencil to her chin and tapped it a few more times, gazing at the ceiling in thought. "Yet, if one approached the endeavor *as* a craftsman with a specific aesthetic goal—perhaps."

Mrs. Haycraft blinked twice. "It's just a thing my father used to say."

"A joke of a fashion." Rose pursed her lips. "Ah! I see."

The housekeeper nodded, her well-humored face reassembling itself into a jovial countenance once again. "That's it."

Rose glanced at her notes. "You were the first to discover the results of the break-in this morning? Is that correct?"

"I did! Came down to start the morning baking as usual. The entire bottom floor was a frightful mess. Broken dishes and crockery strewn about, helter-skelter. And would you believe it? All covered in flour. Looked like it'd snowed. I wonder—"

Rose interrupted, "You must have seen footprints, then."

The woman sat back in her chair. "Didn't think to look, Miss. All I could think of was how angry Mrs. VanderHelm was going to be. You wouldn't want to see her when she's worked up. She's a force of nature." She shook her head, her eyes wide as though seeing a rising thunderstorm driving across a hayfield.

"Surely, the police found prints."

Mrs. Haycraft drew her face into a pinched expression and blew out a puff of air. "Like I said. I was so worried about Mrs. VanderHelm's reaction, that I set to cleaning the place as quick as I could."

"An unfortunate decision for the investigation, but your actions show an admirable attention to cleanliness."

The woman brightened at that. "Why thank you, Miss. That's kind of you. Can't say the police were as understanding or as complimentary."

"I would imagine not." Rose made a note to ask her friend, Detective Donahue, about the possibility of footprints found outside the home.

Mrs. Haycraft leaned forward. "I've never heard of a lady investigator. Must be an interesting job. Did you get that cut on your forehead chasing down a criminal?"

Rose touched her temple. "It was in the line of my professional investigations."

"I envy you, living an exciting life. Makes me proud to be a woman. Here we are, coming into the new century and all. To think we've only had the right to vote for seven years. Hard to believe, ain't it? And here you are, a detective. Who'd have thought it possible? Can you just imagine the future for women?"

"I do, often," Rose said. "Now, tell me what you can about the stolen vase. For example, where was it last night when you retired to your private quarters?"

"That's strange, isn't it? I can think of quite a few other things

I'd have made off with, if I was of a mind to. But I'd never think of doing such a thing." She brought her hand to her breast. "Never!"

"No one is suggesting that at this time, Mrs. Haycraft."

"At this time? Oh, my!" The housekeeper pointed to the teacup in front of Rose and asked, "Are you going to drink that?"

"Probably not." Rose handed the cup to the woman, who gulped down the tepid tea in two swallows.

"What did you ask me?"

Rose glanced at her notes. "Where was the vase when you retired?"

Mrs. Haycraft licked her lips and dropped her hands to her lap. "Mrs. VanderHelm asked me to put it out of sight. She was that much offended by it. She said I should give it some useful function in the kitchen. I intended to store root vegetables in it later this fall."

"But when did you last see it?"

"Let me see. Last night as I was about to turn in. I tucked it in just inside the door of the pantry. When I turned off the light, I forgot it was there and stubbed my little toe on the dreadful thing. Hurt like the dickens."

"So, you're sure that's where it was last night?"

"I can show you my poor toe if you like." She began to remove her shoe.

"That's unnecessary, Mrs. Haycraft." Rose tapped her pencil against her palm. "About the delivery of the vase. Did you receive it?"

"Toby told me there was a delivery man at the front door when I was making biscuits for the noon meal. I didn't hear the man ringing the bell. Think my hearing is going, you know?"

"Who is Toby?" Rose wrote *Toby* on the next page.

"He's the gardener. Also, the handyman. Nice young man. Hard worker."

"So, Toby came to tell you there was a deliveryman at the door." Rose feared the woman might take a tangent with her description of the gardener, a man she obviously viewed favorably. She made a note.

"Yes. Toby wasn't someone the deliveryman thought he could leave a package with. So, he called me."

"Was this a delivery service you were familiar with? Was there anything unusual about the delivery or the man himself?"

The housekeeper wrinkled her brow and didn't answer immediately. "I didn't know the man. But the return address was from an auction house here in Denver. Mrs. VanderHelm has purchased a few things from them over the years, so I recognized the name. McAllister and Sons. All wrapped up nicely. Came in a small wooden trunk, kind of like those china dolls come in. You know the one's that open and look like they're little closets with hangars for the doll's clothes inside? 'Course there weren't any doll clothes or hangars. But it was small like that with the vase packed inside."

"Hmm. What happened to the trunk and wrapping?" Rose asked.

"I think the wrapping paper is still in the trash bin outside, along with what I cleaned up from the kitchen. Do you want to see it?"

"Later, perhaps. What about the trunk?"

"Oh, that's right over here." Mrs. Haycraft pushed herself from her chair and stepped to the far side of the kitchen. "Here it is. I'm using it to store the teapot cozies. I liked it so much, I asked to have use of it."

Rose followed the woman to the counter, waiting to inspect it until the housekeeper had removed the linens stacked within.

The box was a perfect miniature of a traditional steamer trunk, only eighteen inches long. Sweet childhood memories flooded back of ribbons scented with lavender and the texture of lace. It so resembled her own doll's trunk she looked within and half-expected to see her own porcelain doll smiling up at her with painted lips, still dressed in an organdy frock with a ruffled pinafore. She traveled for a moment through a sea of pleasant memories, those shared with her sister Casey. They'd played for hours and set their dolls on grand adventures.

"Any clues that the police missed, Miss McKenzie?"

At the sound of Mrs. VanderHelm's voice, Rose closed the trunk.

The woman clutched Dr. Whitman's arm as though he were a child threatening to fly from her grip. "Has your investigation resulted in any revelations?"

"A few interesting pieces to the puzzle have come to light."

"I'm pleased to hear it," she said, as though Rose had casually commented on the weather and not a break-in to her home. "Your

Dr. Whitman has revealed that his knowledge extends beyond medicine to the botanical world. We completed our tour of the garden, and he has solved a mystery that has puzzled me for the past two years. My mulberry tree has refused to produce fruit. Dr. Whitman reminded me I needed to plant a male of the species to affect a harvest. I blush to admit that I hadn't recalled that bit of botanical advice."

"It's a common mistake," Dr. Whitman said.

Mrs. VanderHelm lifted her chin and formed a severe expression of disapproval. "If I had hired an experienced gardener, he would have known."

Rose did not address the botanical revelations but lifted the small trunk from the counter. "May I take this with me? It may offer further evidence upon deeper inspection."

"Surely, if it might reveal any plausible answer to our mystery."

"May I keep the attorney's letter as well?" Rose asked.

"Of course. This may prove to be an interesting diversion. The social calendar in early fall is rather abysmal. Tiresome charity fund raisers, not at all entertaining." She smiled and squeezed the doctor's arm. "Having you as part of the investigation makes it even more delightful."

Dr. Whitman patted her hand and slipped from her grip, taking a step closer to Rose. "I'm only here to assist as I'm able. It's still Miss McKenzie's investigation."

It gratified Rose to see Mrs. VanderHelm's expression alter. She gave Rose a genuine smile of what was surely approval. "Yes, of course it is."

THE CASE OF THE PECULIAR INHERITANCE

Now that the woman's attention again focused on the case, Rose directed her question to the housekeeper. "Mrs. Haycraft, how was the letter from the attorney attached to the package?"

The woman blinked. "No letter came with it. It didn't come until the next day by regular post. It was Lillian who received it."

"Lillian?"

Mrs. Haycraft looked baffled for a moment before answering, "Oh, that's right. You haven't met her. She's my assistant. Does most of the cleaning outside the kitchen. That's my domain."

"I see. You're sure it came the day after they delivered the package?"

Mrs. Haycraft wrinkled her brow. "Yes, pretty sure. You'll have to talk to Lillian about that, but you might need to come back tomorrow. She's feeling a bit under the weather. Woke up this morning with a terrible stomachache."

Dr. Whitman asked, "Would she like for me to attend to her?"

Mrs. Haycraft waved a hand and shook her head. "Oh, I wouldn't bother. Lillian has a naturally nervous stomach. That's all. She's a high-strung young lady. I'm sure she'll be better tomorrow."

"Well then, we can make the exhibit at the Natural History Museum after all," Dr. Whitman said before Rose could object, and after thanking the two ladies for their hospitality, he steered her for the front door.

CHAPTER 3

Dr. Whitman's buggy zigzagged through the crowded avenue as he navigated delivery wagons and streetcars filled with weekend shoppers.

Rose mentally inventoried each aspect of the case, starting and ending with the only interesting fact—the theft of a vase her client deemed worthless. A crime without a motive was, of course, impossible.

"The vase must have more value than Mrs. VanderHelm suggests." Rose grabbed for the side of the buggy as the doctor tugged sharply on the reins, causing the buggy's right wheel to bounce onto the curb and back down again onto the street with a neck-wrenching jolt.

The doctor yelled out, "Stay on your own side of the road!"

Rose retrieved her bag from the floor. "If only I had a picture of the vase, I could study it more carefully. Mrs. VanderHelm could easily have mistaken the value of the piece. She is highly opinionated, after all. Why wasn't the crime scene secured? The police made most of those prints outside the back door. Heaven only knows what we might have learned about the thief if we could have made a cast of his prints—his size, weight, even his height, certainly his shoe size."

She wagged her finger at no one in particular as she emphasized her point. "There's another reason to take photographs at every crime scene. A photographer could have preserved the evidence on film before half-dozen police officers trampled it." This time, she directed her comment to the doctor. "One day, every police department will hire a photographer for that very purpose. Mark my words."

The doctor said, "That would exceed the budgets of most police departments."

A rapidly approaching delivery cart caused the doctor to swerve in front of a hansom cab. The driver of the cab shook his fist and shouted something indiscernible, and the doctor grumbled, "They should use the alleyways for deliveries, not the main street."

Rose braced her hand against the front of the buggy as it swayed violently left and then sharply right. "What do you make of the one-day delay in delivery of the lawyer's letter?"

"Hold on!" The doctor pulled on the left rein, the buggy narrowly missing a collision with an oncoming streetcar.

Rose frowned. "It is far more likely for a letter of notification to precede the delivery. Don't you agree?"

"No, you don't!" Dr. Whitman slapped the reins against the horse's rump and maneuvered the buggy into a narrow opening in front of the museum. The action prompted another irate reaction from the driver, one the doctor contemptuously ignored. Dr. Whitman jumped out of the buggy and handed the reins and some currency to a waiting attendant.

Rose looked up at the three-story stone building, festooned with a banner announcing **The Pharoah's Final Journey**. To stroll through the museum and search for secrets from the past was one of her favorite ways to spend an afternoon. It satisfied her intellectual curiosity. Maybe she could put aside the case, especially since it offered little mental stimulation, and enjoy the doctor's pleasant company for a few hours.

Dr. Whitman extended to her both a winsome smile and his firm hand. "Shall we?"

A LANKY BOY dressed in a baggy Russian tunic and knickers tugged at his companion's sleeve. "Did you hear the man? He said they stuffed the pharaoh's heart in that jar and his innards in one like that one over there."

Rose stepped around the boys, moving closer to the heavy rope separating visitors from the exhibits. She read the sign before the display of ornate canopic jars and waved for the doctor to join her. "Look at this, Dr. Whitman. Wouldn't you have found a position as a surgeon in Egypt fascinating? In such a culture, there would have been so many opportunities for your studies of anatomy."

Dr. Whitman, still reading the descriptions, didn't respond immediately. "The beauty of the containers certainly conceals the grizzly nature of their contents."

"I think it demonstrates the Egyptians' high regard for death. This elaborate process of preserving the body would indicate that.

Don't you agree?"

"High regard for death? I'm not sure what that means in this context, Miss McKenzie. How can one look upon death with any regard? Surely, it's something natural, but to be avoided at all costs. I'd prefer to think of my high regard for life."

Rose moved a few feet to her right and leaned over the rope, attempting to read the smaller notations on the exhibit. "Oh, my! Do you know how they used this instrument?"

He leaned forward, studying the tool. "It appears to be a simple hook, but I rather doubt ladies used them to button their sandals."

Rose nodded. "Yes. Oh, this is most interesting. I read about this in an archeological article a few years ago. I wish I'd kept it."

The boys had squeezed themselves into the narrow space between an older couple and Rose, expectant young scholars, eager to attend to her explanations.

"The canopic jars, as you know," Rose spoke to the taller boy who listened with his mouth agape. "were used to hold the body organs of the deceased. The stomach, intestines, and liver the Egyptians considered essential in the afterlife, each one carefully extracted and preserved. The heart, however, they left in the body." She directed her question to the boys. "Do you know why?"

Both boys shook their heads and anticipated something deliciously gruesome.

"You see? They considered the heart the seat of the soul and therefore needed for the journey to the afterlife." Rose pursed her lips at the sparse exhibit. "There is much left to conjecture. One of their many mysteries is why they did not preserve the brain. Why the heart but not the brain? What does that tell us about their perceptions of the connection between mind and body, I wonder?"

Dr. Whitman lifted an eyebrow and said, "Careful, Miss McKenzie, before you cross the line between the analytical and the emotional conjectures."

"If I had my choice to travel to an afterlife with only one, it would certainly be the brain," Rose said.

The doctor gave her a wry smile. "That is no revelation, Miss McKenzie."

Rose ignored him and addressed the boys. "But they did not choose the brain."

"Jupiter! Is that true, lady?"

"Absolutely, young man. The hook they placed at the ethmoid bone near the nose." Rose touched the side of the older boy's nose to indicate the location. "It pierced the skull." She demonstrated with a sharp upward stab close to the boy's nose. The boy stepped back with a gasp. "And extracted the brain through the nostrils." Rose brought her hands to her hips, pleased with the effect of her explanations on her young audience.

"Creepers!" the younger boy whispered.

A woman, who had been listening behind them, gave a low moan and collapsed to the floor.

Dr. Whitman responded and attended to the stricken woman. "Will someone fetch a glass of water?"

In a hushed voice, the older boy asked Rose, "You aren't just telling stories?"

"No, young man, I do not tell stories. Ever."

"Jupiter!"

"It is true, is it not, that I do not tell falsehoods regarding science?" Rose asked Dr. Whitman, surprised to see him, along with an older man, assisting a middle-aged woman to her feet.

Dr. Whitman suggested the couple sit for a while on a nearby bench. He moved closer to Rose and whispered, "Honestly, Rose, prudence is not your strong suit."

"What do you mean? I was explaining what the curators have not. The display scarcely touches on the impressive nature of the embalming process. The more fascinating details are sorely lacking."

"Perhaps that was for a reason, considering the fact that your elucidations caused the woman to faint."

Rose lifted her chin a mild degree. "Some women swoon at the sight of blood, even though they witness a flow of it every month of their childbearing years. I do not understand it."

Dr. Whitman gripped her arm and led her from the gathering crowd. When they had located a quiet corner behind a provocative plaster cast of a statue of Nefertari, he pulled up, then drew in a heavy breath. "Rose, seriously, you just can't burst out with every thought or opinion that pops into your head."

"I was explaining the Egyptian process of preparing their dead for the afterlife. It's all there on display."

He rolled his eyes. "But you described it in such detail—you practically demonstrated it."

Rose frowned. "You don't approve of me."

Dr. Whitman sighed and ran a hand down his face, holding it over his mouth for another minute. "That's not true. I have the highest regard for you. You're one of the most intelligent and insightful women I have ever known."

Rose opened her mouth, but Dr. Whitman held up a finger to silence her.

"You are more intelligent and well-read than most of my male colleagues. You have incredible foresight, and one day, I have no doubt you will command the respect of a wider audience than this humble doctor, who is still your friend."

"But you don't approve of my frankness."

He rubbed a hand across the back of his neck, then dropped it to his side and stared at her for another extended moment. "Sometimes. Sometimes you could try to temper your frankness with a little restraint. Be sensitive to those around you."

Rose studied him, sorting through the probability of his opinions being accurate. His obvious discomfort bothered her. She lifted her eyes to the voluptuous figure towering above them. Dr. Whitman followed her gaze. "Did you know Nefertari was only fifteen when she married and that she co-reigned Egypt with her husband?" Rose traced the statue with her eye for precision, stopping at the statue's delicate toe. She reached up, patted the statue's shapely calf, and said, "With fashion designers so focused on the female bosom, I cannot understand why a woman's leg, which is of equal beauty in line and form, remains concealed from the public eye. In this modern age, one would think fashion to keep abreast of changing perceptions of feminine modesty. It's a shame."

Rose broke from her revelry and lay her hand on the doctor's arm. "I'm famished. Let's have lunch."

CHAPTER 4

Rose skewered a slice of ham, scrutinized it a few inches from her eye, then lay her fork on her plate. "Why is it clients only come to me with cases for missing things—missing dogs, missing husbands, missing jewelry, missing vases?" She propped her chin in her palm. "Casey's probably off chasing down a member of some notorious band of outlaws through Wyoming or posing as an actress in some saloon to spy on a forger."

Dr. Whitman pushed his own plate aside. "Do I see a tint of green in those blue eyes?"

"I'm bored."

"For the moment." He refused the waitress's offer to refill his coffee cup. "Besides, you still haven't solved the case you have now. It's a puzzle, isn't it, and you like puzzles?"

"It was probably one of the staff. The housekeeper had opportunity and means. Unlike Mrs. VanderHelm, she might have liked the vase. In that case, she could have pinched it."

"Pinched it? Have you been reading Dickens again?"

Rose waved her hand, dismissing the comment, and frowned at the remnants of her dismembered sandwich. "It's the unanswered questions surrounding the man who bequeathed the gift and his connection to the client that's more interesting."

"There you go. You need to investigate the mysterious Mr. Larson."

"I hate it when you patronize me."

"I'm not patronizing you."

"You are, and you don't even attempt to pretend otherwise," Rose said sullenly.

"You get like this whenever you compare yourself to your sister."

"It is true. She gets the thrilling cases and I get—a missing ugly vase."

"But there might be more to it than what it appears. Maybe there's a map to a missing gold mine. There are enough stories still circulating about lost mines that one day we are certain to read of one's discovery. I wouldn't be surprised if gold veins wove beneath High Street."

Rose ran her finger along the painted blue edge of her plate and thought about the tombs of Egyptian pharaohs and secrets undiscovered. "I need to find out more about the man who died. Raymond Larson. Who was he? Did Mrs. VanderHelm know him by another name? Was there some message etched into the ceramic?"

"Or a map to his lost gold mine or a treasure of stolen Confederate gold? Think like a writer of fiction."

Rose tapped her fingernail against the plate. "It's creative thinking combined with solid facts that solve any investigation.

One has to consider a wider scope of scenarios, then systematically sort and discard those not supported by the facts."

"So, you're considering the possibility that the vase had more value than Mrs. VanderHelm has ascribed to it."

"Or there was something in the vase," she said.

"But why send it to Mrs. VanderHelm?"

"I must talk to the delivery company. Perhaps he simply delivered it to the wrong address." Rose pushed back from the table and picked up her wrap. "I'm returning to my study."

Dr. Whitman scrambled to his feet, reached for his cup, and finished the lukewarm coffee before running after her.

ONLY A SLIGHT draft slipped around the edge of the heavy fabric Mrs. Pennyworth had hung to cover the broken window in Rose's study. The bulky fisherman's sweater Rose had pulled over her shirtwaist made the cool evening breeze seeping into the room scarcely noticeable. Rose concluded the colder air sharpened her wits.

At the top of the chalkboard hanging on the opposite wall, Rose had written: **The Case of the Peculiar Inheritance.** Beneath were the words **Means, Opportunity, Motive.** She pressed her teeth into her lower lip. Under the first and second category, she wrote the names of each member of Mrs. VanderHelm's staff.

"But where is the motive, Sergeant?" Rose let out a deep breath and drew a large question mark. "Why steal something of little value?"

Sergeant lifted one ear before rolling over onto his side and stretching his legs.

With the chalk, Rose tapped a steady rhythm against her chin. "Hmm. It's time to interview the interested parties. Mr. Charles Kent, the attorney for the deceased will be first on my rounds. Then the conveniently absent, Miss Lillian Finnegan."

Sergeant's stomach rumbled.

"I think you may be right, clever boy. The delivery company should be interrogated earlier than later."

Rose scrutinized the board and scowled. "Sergeant, we are woefully lacking clues. I'm convinced there is something quite obvious we are missing."

The hound lifted his head and rolled his eyes in Rose's direction. He showed no intention of moving as she stepped over him to reach the board. She added a name to the empty space. Raymond Larson. She kept her chalk on the letter "n" before writing **Deceased**, followed by another question mark.

"Ah, but did he die a natural death?" That bit of information was unknown to her, but it was certainly relevant to the investigation. A murder... now a murder would hold her interest for quite some time. She almost smiled.

She perched on the stool staring at the board for a time, then closed her eyes. She imagined the darkened kitchen, the vase behind the pantry door, the person kneeling on the back porch, trying his picks in the lock, the click as the lock released, the stealthy opening of the door. The search. A sound. Someone awakens in the house. A creak on the stairs. An urgency to search before discovery. She opened her eyes and focused on the chalkboard, the names sliding from one category to the next, interchanging places in rapid succession. Words appeared like ghosts drawn in white chalk—**Greed, Lust, Hatred, Love**. These were universal motives, but where was the one that defined this case?

The trunk she'd brought back with her sat on the end of the lab table. She ran her hand along the smooth oak grain. Although she'd identified the size and shape as similar to her doll chest, people used them for a variety of purposes. Women took them when traveling to secure their personal items. Men occasionally carried in them papers related to business. It offered convenience, something to tuck beneath one's arm.

A small stamp on the bottom identified the manufacturer in Philadelphia. Apart from normal wear, no nicks or damage appeared. The locking mechanism functioned, but according to the housekeeper it had not come with a key. She lifted the lid, again feeling the nostalgia wash over her as it had earlier. Like her doll chest, this one had a cloth lining, plain and without pattern. Leather hinges were nothing remarkable. There was simply nothing evident to make it interesting to thieves.

With a quick shake of her head, she closed the lid and walked to the wall of bookcases. Sergeant stretched and padded across the room at her heels. Behind a leather volume of *The Professor* by Charlotte Brontë, Rose pulled a lever and the narrow bookcase swung inward to reveal a room of child-like proportions beneath the sloping ceiling. When Rose had discovered the room a few years ago, she'd found evidence that it was a room designed for children. A toy wooden wagon remained, wedged into the low space between ceiling and floor. At the center of the room, whimsical nursery animals woven into an oval carpet created a sense of an eternal parade of bunnies and ducks.

On the far wall, moonlight streamed through an oval dormer window, forming diamond patterns across the coral-colored carpet. Rose lit the oil lamp sitting atop the desk tucked beneath the window. She ducked to avoid striking her head on the low beam and sat on the brocade tuffet, crossing her legs beneath the desk.

Sergeant wedges himself under the table and collapsed with a loud expulsion of air before he rested his head on Rose's feet. The paper within the typewriter displayed a few lines of text, the work of a previously sleepless night. She poised her hands above the keys and waited. Then the scene began inside her head and the words came to her effortlessly, as though she'd lived them.

Cassandra slipped from the saddle and tied her horse to a juniper bush. She moved with utmost stealth, feeling her way along the rock face for the opening she knew must be there. The opening hadn't shown itself before. But this night, the moon guided her. Tonight, she would find the answer. Somewhere in the cave was the hidden entrance to the lost mine.

CHAPTER 5

"Have you seen my sleeve bands?" Rose asked, while sorting through the items populating the pocket of her lab apron.

Mrs. Pennyworth stepped up behind her. "You mean the ones in your skirt pocket here?" She tugged the elastic bands free of Rose's pocket and held them up between her forefinger and thumb.

"Thank you, Mrs. Pennyworth. What would I do without you?"

The housekeeper harrumphed and asked, "Have you been up all night writing again?"

Rose adjusted the band holding the full sleeve of her blouse tight to her forearm. "Not all night, no. I had a chapter I needed to finish." She tugged her jacket over her sleeve.

"You *look* like you've been up all night. Bloodshot eyes and those dark circles give you the appearance of a rabid raccoon."

"I need to go out this morning. Would you ask the neighbor boy to walk Sergeant for me, and please remind him not to walk down Walnut Street. There's a vicious cat there that has an affinity for attacking all dogs and has a particular vendetta against Sergeant."

"Well, it won't have an affinity for long if it isn't more discriminating. Have you seen the new neighbor's wolf? I fear for my life every time I go outside now. If they ever forget to feed the beast breakfast, heaven help me if I need to hang the sheets on the line."

"I'm sure it isn't a wolf. Wolves have proven to make poor domesticated pets."

"Tell the neighbors that." Mrs. Pennyworth picked up the soiled lab apron and draped it over her arm. She squinted at Rose from across the room. "You aren't going out like that, are you?"

Rose looked around at her housekeeper's arched brows and asked, "Why shouldn't I?"

"Because you look like you've been up all night. Your hair's a fright. Did you sleep in that skirt?"

"I'm on a case, Mrs. Pennyworth. You know how it is." Rose crossed the room to the wall mirror and poked ineffectively at her hair. She frowned at her reflection, irritated as usual when Mrs. Pennyworth's observations were better than her own. "I'll change my skirt."

"Don't forget to fix your hair." The housekeeper snagged a discarded pile of rags on her way to the door. "I'll have breakfast ready in short order. Don't dawdle."

Rose, still poking at her hair, called after her, "I don't have time for more than toast and tea."

Mrs. Pennyworth spun, her voice carrying all the weight her

five feet could muster behind it. "Miss Rose McKenzie, you will eat a proper breakfast! I know you won't bother with lunch when you're on a case, so you'll just have to put a move on."

AFTER COMPLYING TO eat one of Mrs. Pennyworth's full breakfasts of eggs, sausage, and toast, Rose rolled her bicycle down the front steps to the street. Dodging Denver's busy morning traffic was a feat of not so much physical agility as mental composure. Mostly, Rose had learned to ignore the angry calls from men driving horse-drawn carts, but the horns still made her flinch. It was disturbing that the men who could be the most gracious and genteel when meeting a woman on the sidewalk turned into absolute beasts when in some wheeled vehicle on the streets.

The four-story stone building in the Highland District made an impressive statement for the success of Mr. Charles Kent's law office. Rose maneuvered her bike up the steps and through the door. However, the lobby offered scarce space for depositing her wheels of transportation.

A young man dressed in an ill-fitting uniform and wearing a box-like hat approached her. "Would you like me to tuck your bicycle next to mine? I make deliveries for the building and found a nice little nook in that closet over there." He pointed to a glass door at the end of the narrow hallway. "Think it used to be an office of some sort, but no one's using it now." He hitched a shoulder and reached for the handlebars. "May I?"

THE CASE OF THE PECULIAR INHERITANCE

"That's very kind of you. Thank you."

"Glad to help a fellow delivery . . ." His cheeks colored. "Delivery lady. You're the first I've met." Before Rose could correct him, the young man doffed his cap and walked off with the bike.

Rose approached the door with the attorney's name painted in neat block letters. She noted that no associates were listed before stepping inside to find a young woman seated behind the reception desk.

"I'm here to see Mr. Kent."

From the style of her hair piled high atop her head, to the crisp, white shirtwaist, the receptionist might have stepped from an illustration by Charles Gibson. This model of the feminine ideal smiled stiffly at her and asked, "What is the nature of your business, Miss?"

"My client, Mrs. Verbena VanderHelm, has employed my services to investigate a matter that involves a letter sent by Mr. Kent to her residence."

The secretary's eyes swept over Rose's five-feet-nine inches, and Rose surmised that along with assessing her stylish attire, the young woman knew exactly the type of bustle and undergarments she wore beneath. From the arch of her meticulously attended eyebrow, Rose guessed she also had a fairly accurate tally of the expense of her entire wardrobe.

"An investigator?" she asked.

"Yes. Will you please let Mr. Kent know I wish a few minutes of his time?"

"Your name, please?"

Rose passed her card to the woman. "Miss Rose McKenzie."

The secretary took her time, flipping the card over and then back again. "Mrs. VanderHelm is also a client of Mr. Kent's. Last spring, she hosted a benefit for the widows of miners. She's a lot nicer than she seems when you first meet her. Under all those ridiculous trappings of her generation, she's just like us. Victoria . . . I mean Mrs. Miller and I attended the event together."

The Gibson Girl look-alike rose to her feet, smoothed her skirt, and extended her hand to Rose. "I'm Cynthia Gaylord. I'll make sure you see Mr. Kent." She leaned across the desk and whispered, "We modern women have to stick together."

True to her word, the secretary escorted Rose into Kent's office a few minutes later, left Rose's card on the desk almost beneath her boss's nose, and closed the door when she exited.

Charles Kent glanced at Rose's business card before looking up again from behind the fortress of his mahogany desk. "An investigator." Rose decided the man should shave his beard, as it gave him an austere appearance which jurors might find objectionable. "You say Mrs. VanderHelm has asked you to investigate what exactly?"

"As a professional, Mr. Kent, I'm sure your clients receive utmost confidentiality. I, too, hold to the same professional standard," Rose said in her practiced level tone.

The man nodded his head, as though he approved of her answer. "How can I help?" He leaned back in his chair, folding his arms. "As long as it doesn't violate *my* clients' confidence."

THE CASE OF THE PECULIAR INHERITANCE

Uncertain if he intended this as wry humor or sarcasm, she ignored his remark. "Mrs. VanderHelm received a letter from your office two days ago, informing her of a gift she would receive as the result of an estate settlement for a Mr. Raymond Larson. Are you familiar with the letter of which I speak?"

He pursed his lips and rolled his eyes to the ceiling, the model expression of a man recalling events from memory. It was also an effective tool for stalling. "Yes, I assist Mrs. VanderHelm occasionally, usually it's financial help she requests. But I don't recall such a letter coming across my desk of late. We're still liquidating Mr. Larson's estate, you see. It may have, and I simply didn't place special attention to it."

"Yes, I see. My father was an attorney, so I understand a little of the process of inheritance and estate management. A sizeable estate can be complex."

At the mention of her father, Kent sat forward and asked, "Did he practice here in Denver?"

"No, in the East." Rose sensed his curiosity and deflected another question with one of her own. "Who would know of the letter? Your secretary?"

"No. Actually, I have a legal assistant specifically assigned to Mr. Larson's estate. She's been handling many of the smaller details. Let me call her in. She may be of help to you."

His energetic stride to the door and the obvious strength of his physique suggested to Rose that he maintained a less sedentary lifestyle than most she knew in the legal profession. Long hours at their desks and little activity led to body styles strikingly different from Mr. Charles Kent. The man's physical similarities to her father struck her, except her father had resisted fads of facial hair for his entire life. Maybe that's why she had a particular dislike for men who preferred to cover their faces like wild animals.

"Miss Gaylord, would you ask Mrs. Miller to come in here, please?" He turned back from the door and perched on the edge of his desk a few feet from Rose. "I hope this isn't offensive, but it sparks my curiosity, and I have to ask. How did you become an investigator, Miss McKenzie? I know certainly that women are challenging their traditional roles, but yours is unique."

"As I said, my father was an attorney. My uncle became a Pinkerton operative after leaving the Chicago police force. So, law enforcement is, you might say, in my blood."

"Ah. I see." He folded his arms across his chest, a gesture Rose recognized as defensive. "I wonder why you choose to follow in your uncle's footsteps instead of your father's."

While Rose had observed men interact with each other for the first time, she found their posturing remarkably like the males of most species. Each would assess the other in a motionless form of dancing, an arching of the back, a squaring of the shoulders, a lift of the chin, all performed wordlessly to appear more imposing than their obvious physical stature conveyed.

But where women were concerned, the rules of engagement were less evolved, as only in recent times had women posed such a threat to the male of the species, even though the nature of the threat was unrealized. So, Rose accepted the man's appraising study of her, something she'd learned to both expect and mostly ignore. She'd also learned the skill of appearing completely placid as they took her measure both of her physicality and intellect.

Kent stated an undeniable fact, and Rose did not detect any tone of acerbity. "Women are making their way into the legal profession, too. Mrs. Miller is an example. She's the first female legal assistant I've employed."

"That's to your credit, Mr. Kent," Rose said with genuine respect.

He acknowledged the compliment with a mild smile in response. "Not as much as you might think. I knew her father, and I agreed based on the belief that any offspring of his would probably be a prodigy. My gamble paid off. She's an excellent assistant, and I believe she'll make an excellent attorney one day. I'm pleased with her work."

There was a light knock on the doorpost. "You wanted to see me, Mr. Kent?" A petite young woman, a full head shorter than Rose, stood in the doorway, her hand still resting on the doorknob.

"Please come in. I'd like you to meet Miss Rose McKenzie. She's an investigator. What is it the Pinkerton's call those in your profession? A private eye?"

Rose suppressed a groan at his use of the loathsome term. She nodded at Mrs. Miller and extended her hand. The woman's grip was soft and uncertain. She, too, gave Rose a quick visual appraisal, different from the man's but serving a similar purpose.

"How may I help you?" the woman asked cordially in a voice as soft as her hand.

Rose pulled the attorney's letter from her handbag and passed it to the younger woman. "Mrs. VanderHelm received this letter notifying her that Mr. Larson had given her a gift as a part of his estate settlement. Do you remember sending it to her?"

With her head down, Rose could not read her face and observe her reaction. This was unfortunate, as Rose had found people's faces often revealed more than their guarded language. People were natural liars, some better than others. It was a view both her father and her uncle shared as devotedly as any religious creed.

Mrs. Miller slowly nodded. "Yes, I believe so. I sent the letter this week."

"Mrs. VanderHelm received it three days ago. Did you know Mr. Larson well?"

Her lips took a slight shift downward, and she responded quickly. "Only in a superficial sense to confirm with him his last wishes regarding the estate. Mr. Kent assigned me to handle the auction of his household goods."

"And distribution of gifts?"

"Oh, yes, his gifts as well. We would consider them a part of the estate and therefore an inheritance," Mrs. Miller said in an official tone reflecting her aspiring position.

Rose resumed questioning Kent. "How long was Mr. Larson your client?"

Kent's brows elevated, and his answer took a little longer than Rose would have expected. Judging from the size of his office and staff, his practice was not so large that he'd not be intimately familiar with each client. "I believe I've been handling his legal matters for the past six or seven years."

"Did he ever mention Mrs. VanderHelm to either of you?" Rose asked.

Charles Kent shrugged. "He was a very private person. I had the impression he had few close friends, only associates. Our job was to notify and distribute his estate. Regarding his relationships with these individuals, I'm afraid that neither Mrs. Miller nor I could comment."

"What type of business allowed Mr. Larson to gain such a sizeable estate?"

Kent hesitated for the briefest of moments, perhaps weighing the possibility of violating his position of client confidentiality. "A variety of enterprises. More recently, I believe he did well in land investments."

The brevity of his answer gave Rose the impression confidentiality won out over clarity. He glanced up at the handsome Sheffield wall clock and said, "Unfortunately, we have an appointment for which to prepare. I'm sorry we weren't more helpful."

Accepting her cue, Rose gathered her gloves and bag. "Not at all. You've been very kind to see me without an appointment. Thank you." She rose to her feet, extending her hand to the attorney.

Kent took her hand, and Rose gathered from his somewhat surprised expression that it startled him to see they stood eye-to-eye. The surprise relaxed into a warm smile and he said, "If Mrs. Miller can answer any more of your questions, please don't hesitate to ask."

The young woman echoed her employer's offer. "Whatever I can do to help, Miss McKenzie."

Releasing Rose's hand, the attorney opened the door for her. Instead of a formal goodbye, he said cheerfully, "Good luck."

Rose asked, "One more question. Who is handling the auction of his household goods?"

Mrs. Miller opened the file and flipped through several pages. "McAllister and Sons."

"Thank you." Rose nodded to the Gibson Girl secretary, who winked at her as she passed from the office.

Although she'd not received what she'd hoped from the attorney, she left with another point of contact. Perhaps Mr. McAllister could provide some description of the vase and its estimated value. It was still possible Mrs. VanderHelm had misjudged the gift's value. If that was true, the theft became less of a mystery and more decidedly a crime. She experienced only the slightest twinge of guilt at hoping for the latter.

It was a lovely fall day, so Rose walked her bike along the sidewalk for the four miles from the Highland business district back to Mrs. VanderHelm's house in Lincoln park. She enjoyed the bustle of the city and could think clearly when not dodging streetcars and delivery carts. As she strolled, she allowed her mind time to review the few facts she had gathered.

As cooperative as Kent had been, his claim to client

confidentiality severely limited the information she might glean by direct questioning. Her father had commented on the frustration he experienced when he knew of a client's involvement in some criminal activity, and it bound him to silence due to their professional relationship. Those were the rare times he would disappear into his study and close the door, shutting out the girls from his cheerful company.

Of necessity, then, knowledge of Mrs. VanderHelm's benefactor would come from another source. Mrs. Miller, of course, might be privy to details of Mr. Larson's business relationships, but Rose refused to compromise the young woman's position as his law clerk. Just as Kent upheld his client's expectation for privacy, she had a professional obligation to her employer.

But who else? There was Detective Donahue. He'd helped her before, gaining access to information not intended for the public eye. If Raymond Larson had a criminal record, surely the sergeant would know of it, and with a little persuasion he might even share it.

First, she would interview the housemaid with the nervous stomach. With her next steps planned and encouraged to learn if there was some more interesting criminal aspect to the case, Rose climbed onto her bike and took her chances in the uncivilized street. Excluding any unfortunate close encounter with horses or streetcars, she'd be at Mrs. VanderHelm's door in minutes.

CHAPTER 6

As Rose rode onto the brick drive leading to the grand house, Mrs. Haycraft trotted down the front steps of the expansive porch, fluttering her arms. "Oh, Mrs. VanderHelm will be glad to see you, Miss. She's been pacing in the back garden for hours. Won't let Lillian or me in the kitchen until you've finished your detecting. We're all half-starved."

"Why? What's happened?" Rose propped her bike against the porch railing and waited while the housekeeper caught her breath.

"Someone broke in again last night. Didn't make the mess like the night before, but they broke a window this time. Glass all over the sink."

Rose started up the steps at a trot. "Have you called the police?"

"Oh, no! Mrs. VanderHelm said they made such a mess of it yesterday that she only trusted you to inspect for clues. I'd be more excited if I weren't so hungry. Will your detecting take long?"

"I shall do my best to work with a thought for expediency, Mrs.

Haycraft."

A quick visual examination revealed the point of entry. Unlike yesterday, the intruder had broken the window over the kitchen sink. The curtain lay half in the basin, suggesting this entry was made by someone without knowledge of how to pick a lock.

Rose carefully brushed away shards of broken window glass to allow closer inspection of the windowsill. On the wooden casing, a smear of blood colored a glass fragment still embedded in the frame, and Rose could almost hear the intruder swear.

Such evidence suggested inexperience because a professional would have worn gloves. Gingerly lifting the curtain, it gratified her to find not one but two crimson fingerprints stamped on the bleached muslin.

The amount of glass on the counter indicated the intruder had not left the way he'd entered. She glanced to the back door, the one that had been so expertly picked the night before. On closer inspection, she found another streak of dried blood on the door's handle. "Hmm."

She straightened and scanned the immediate area. The ingress and egress were clear, plus she had two prints to study. Things were looking up.

Mrs. Haycraft's voice called to her from across the room. Rose stood in the doorway, careful not to venture into the kitchen and said, "Wonder why they were so neat this time. No broken dishes or throwing my pantry goods around the place. It's odd, when you think that none of us heard him the first time, but this time Lillian did."

"Anything taken?"

Mrs. Haycraft shrugged. "Not that we can tell, but Mrs. VanderHelm was quite clear that we not mess around in here, cleaning and disturbing the clues."

Rose wished the woman had complied with her employer's wishes more judiciously, since the intruder had not necessarily confined himself to the kitchen. "Please retrace your steps to the front door. You may unknowingly have destroyed more evidence."

"Oh! Sorry!" Mrs. Haycraft began a slow backward walk to the front door.

Sunlight streamed through eastern windows and created a sparkling trail of glass shards from the broken window to the pantry. Inside was limited proof that the intruder had been searching for something but with more care than the night before. Rose's abilities to retain both images and written material with photographic clarity served her well now. Canned and boxed goods were clearly not as well ordered as she'd noted yesterday. Thankfully, Mrs. Haycraft kept her kitchen in meticulous order.

Rose dropped to her knees and followed the trail of glass. The rug inside the dining room made her job more challenging, but there were enough pieces to suggest the intruder searched this room as well. Only the women of the house could determine if something was missing. Satisfied that she'd found all the obvious evidence, she invited Mrs. Haycraft and Mrs. VanderHelm inside the house.

"I'd like you to thoroughly search these rooms for anything

that might be missing but don't touch anything. Note any item out of place, no matter how small. We seem to have an extremely picky thief. If you come up with something, find me."

"Where will you be?" Mrs. VanderHelm asked.

"I want to check for footprints outside." Rose headed toward the kitchen again, then asked, "Didn't Mrs. Haycraft say that Lillian heard the intruder this time?"

"She did. Seems she scared him off this time. Makes me quite anxious to think the house can be broken into with such ease. I may need to hire a guard." The woman reached for Rose's arm. "Or should I buy a gun, do you think?"

Rose had an alarming image of Mrs. VanderHelm wielding a weapon. "I'm not sure that's necessary, but arming a member of your staff, perhaps." As she considered the image of the housekeeper facing down an intruder with a shotgun, she was no less frightful. "Perhaps, at your request, you might convince the police to patrol the neighborhood with more diligence."

"Yes! That's an excellent suggestion. I know the mayor well enough to earn an audience."

"May I speak with Lillian as soon as possible?"

From across the room, Mrs. Haycraft called back over her shoulder, "That girl went straight back to bed when we discovered the broken window. I'll go fetch her."

Rose stood on the doorstep studying the dirt on either side of the stoop. There appeared to be a slight print on the left side. Still, a clear print might be outside the broken window.

She was kneeling in the grass, carefully spreading the blades of grass, when someone gave a small cry of exclamation from the other side of the house. Curious, Rose jumped to her feet and quietly made her way to the source of the sound where she surreptitiously peered around the corner. A young woman clung to a trellis about halfway between the first and second floors where she was frantically tugging at her skirt, snagged on the rose vine.

The woman looked over at Rose and with a grunt jerked the fabric free, jumping the final few feet to the ground. She then made a dash for the street where a cabbie waited in a horse-drawn cab.

"Lillian, I must speak with you!" Rose called out to her while sprinting to catch up, but the woman didn't stop until she threw herself into the cab. They were off before Rose could reach the sidewalk. Without stopping to catch her breath, Rose sprinted for the front of the house. There she retrieved her bike and pedaled after the cab.

Rose raced to the side street in time to see the cab turn in a direction that blessedly would take them downhill instead of up. She might have a chance of catching up, accelerating with less effort as gravity drew her inexorably down. Unfortunately, this street had been designed with an eye for aesthetics, yielding to stands of large leaf maples spaced randomly in her path. Rose had read of Norwegian slalom competitions where men raced down hills weaving a treacherous course through trees. Surely, she could accomplish the same without the snow. Refusing to contemplate what might happen to her body should she miss one bend in the road and collide with one immovable tree, she continued to add to her considerable speed by pedaling. She felt momentary gratitude that the cab had taken a route through the residential neighborhood instead of city traffic, where she'd be dodging horses and trees.

Incredibly, the cab remained in sight with the gap clearly closing between them. While a portion of her brain worked out the physics of keeping her bike upright, another endeavored to recall the street map of Denver posted on her study wall. Only a few blocks east and south was a district of boarding houses and eating establishments for Denver's residents, not numbered among the privileged who'd found or inherited wealth from the golden years of mining.

It was probable Lillian raced there now. If she evaded Rose, it would be a challenge to ferret her out of the safe environs of family and friends. She could easily disappear into an entire square block of Finnegans, O'Haras, and Kellys. The possibility of losing her spurred Rose to lean into the wind screaming past her ears.

Had she not removed her hat inside Mrs. VanderHelm's parlor, she'd have lost it by now. But Rose fought to keep strands of hair from obscuring her view, batting at them with one hand while fighting to maintain balance with the other. "Blazes!" Wind ripped the curse from her lips.

As she'd guessed, a block ahead, the cab turned south. Her own speed dropped as the road leveled out, making the turn less harrowing. She straightened her back and her front tire. The sudden appearance of traffic quickly extinguished any elation she might have experienced surviving the descent. Streetcar rails dividing the thoroughfare forced other modes of transportation into the narrow lanes on either side. Horse-drawn carts and carriages jostled for space, while daring or oblivious pedestrians dashed across the street like rabbits.

She gauged the distance between the woman's cab and her bicycle as less than a block. Her thighs burning with the effort, she pumped even harder. An opening appeared between a wide milk wagon and a two-wheeled cart. She calculated the seconds the wagon would overtake the cart. Five at most. She could squeeze within the opening in three seconds, only four as long as neither altered their speed. She sped ahead, watching for her moment. She leaned sharply left and drove through the narrow space, bruising the knuckles of her left hand on the wagon's rough exterior. As she cut back in front of the horse, the driver let loose a string of profane words uttered in Italian.

Now, close enough to the cab, she could see the side of the young woman's face as she stared incredulously over her shoulder at Rose. If the young woman escaped, that quick glimpse of her face should allow Rose to recognize her again.

A horn blared from a horseless carriage. She jerked her attention away from the woman and back to the traffic blocking her way. With the ice wagon ahead of her and the approaching streetcar, Rose calculated her own speed. From her vantage, the length of the wagon was impossible to factor into her calculations. It would be necessary to pass the truck before the streetcar reached them. Indisputably, the space could not accommodate her and the bike.

Rose swallowed hard and sped forward, moving to the left between the tracks and the left wheel of the wagon. The wagon was longer than she's expected, by at least five feet. Her legs pumped harder, her heart hammering in protest against her ribs. She glanced up to see the streetcar driver's wide-eyed alarm just as she jerked the bike to the right and around the team of horses. Another oath assaulted her, this time the words carried a distinctly Irish brogue and at greater volume than the Italian's.

She scanned the vehicles ahead, no longer seeing the cab. As a man on horseback turned his animal from the curb into the lane of traffic, Rose caught sight of the familiar black cab turning right at the next intersection. She slipped into the space the man and his horse had vacated and bounced up onto the sidewalk, precipitating another angry shout, this time from a boy selling papers. Rose shouted an apology as he leaped aside to escape her front tire.

A few feet more and she narrowly avoided another collision with two women lost in conversation and oblivious to the bicycle careening toward them. Deciding her chances were better in the street, she bounced off the curb just ahead of another horse and wagon. Less than half a block separated her from the cab. If her lungs didn't burst, her skirt stayed free of the spinning wheel, and she could pass the only wagon separating them, a chance remained.

Neither of those catastrophes fell upon her. Unfortunately, the one thing she could not avoid was the mountain of horse manure left by street cleaners suddenly looming in her path. At the speed she was traveling, she didn't have a chance. Blocked on either side by wagons, there was no recourse but to plow through it and hope for the best.

She remembered very little after her front tire spun left and the bike slid sideways. The tires performed like shovels, slipping beneath the pile, taking Rose with them in a trajectory toward the streetcar tracks.

CHAPTER 7

Dr. Whitman gently manipulated Rose's ankle. "Does that hurt?" he asked.

"Of course, it hurts. It's badly sprained, which naturally creates a contusion, hence the swelling, thereby the pain. But you could tell that by looking at it and not inflicting further injury to my appendage by twisting it." Rose muttered the last through clenched teeth.

He countered her bitter response by giving her a sympathetic grin, saying, "You're a terrible patient." Picking up a strip of linen cut from Mrs. Pennyworth's worn apron, he gently wrapped her rapidly coloring ankle. "It seems our relationship is conditional to your injuries," he said, the earlier sympathy replaced by a mischievous twinkle in his eye. "Which, much to my good fortune, is nearly a weekly event of late. You could simply invite me to dinner, you know."

Rose pushed herself back into the cushions of her chair and said sullenly, "My beautiful new bike is ruined."

"Mrs. Pennyworth told me it slid under the wheels of the streetcar. It's good for everyone you'd fallen off by then into something—soft." His tone altered from humor to disapproval. "Honestly, Rose, you behave more like your sister every day. You'll be scaling buildings, tripping across rooftops, and jumping off trains next."

"Do you think so?" she said, brightening.

He drew in a deep breath and shook his head. "They have trained your sister, Casey, for what she does as a Pinkerton."

She sunk back into the chair cushions. "I lost her."

"Who? Your sister?"

Rose scowled at him, "Of course not. Lillian Finnegan, Mrs. VanderHelm's housemaid. I lost her when I crashed."

"I see."

Rose noticed that the doctor's stroking of her ankle created a most pleasant sensation.

"Why were you chasing the housemaid?"

"Because she ran."

"Oh. That explains it," he said, his lips twitching with amusement.

Rose dropped her arms to either side of the chair, slipping lower into the cushions, surprised at her fatigue. "Unfortunately, she prevailed and escaped my pursuit. But the good news is that Detective Donahue might know her family or at least a contingent of them."

"Detective Donahue? When did you see him?"

"Fortunately for me, he was in the neighborhood on his own investigation. He's the one who brought me home." Her voice fell an octave as she added, "Along with what's left of my cycle." She tugged at a loose thread protruding from the pillow's seam, recalling the details of their conversation. "He also promised to find out more about Raymond Larson, the man who gave the vase to Mrs. VanderHelm."

"I can help with that."

"How?"

"I have relevant information about your Mr. Larson."

Rose shifted her position, while keeping her ankle on the doctor's knee. "Tell me."

"I heard my colleague, Dr. Sheffield, speaking of an autopsy in which he assisted. The body was that of Raymond Larson."

This was news she could use. "Why an autopsy? Did the police suspect his death was not of natural causes?"

Dr. Whitman nodded. "The coroner found no apparent evidence of violent death, but the police had their suspicions after consideration of his nefarious business dealings."

"What kind of nefarious? Did he say?"

"No. He made some assumptions based on the questions asked by the police. I think they suspected poisoning. They also asked if he could have been suffocated. I found that question puzzling."

"Intriguing," Rose said.

"Their suspicions apparently gave them enough reason to search his house for evidence of foul play."

"Hmm. You have been a busy detective. This is enlightening information, doctor."

"Glad to be of service."

"It opens up an entirely new line of possibilities, doesn't it?"

Rose looked down at her ankle, then up at the doctor. "Why did you stop?"

Dr. Whitman smiled and resumed his massage. "I think it strongly suggests he was not of the same society circle as Mrs. VanderHelm. Unless she's hiding something from us, I can't imagine when they would have been in the same room together, let alone discuss a similar fascination for porcelain vases."

"Excellent point." Rose closed her eyes, wondering if all doctors knew how to give massages. She felt a delicious heaviness in her limbs. Half-awake, she said, "There was a second break-in last night at Mrs. VanderHelm's home."

"What did they steal this time? The rolling pin?"

Rose opened her eyes, squinting at the doctor. "Of course, not! Why would they do that?"

Dr. Whitman lowered her ankle and sat back, shaking his head. "That was a joke."

"Oh." Rose tried to discern the humor in his comment but gave up, resuming her narrative of the day's events. "Unless Mrs. VanderHelm hasn't notified me, she and her housekeeper could find nothing missing. But this one was a forced entry through the window. The would-be thief was unusually fastidious while searching."

"Nothing stolen? Maybe they were scared off?"

"That's a plausible answer." She shook her head to clear it and sat up, staring at a spot on the wall just over the doctor's shoulder. "What I find striking is that the patterns of the break-ins were vastly different. I don't think it was the same person. In fact, I still think this second one was just one individual. It's difficult to know that about the first due to the destruction of evidence by the police."

"What makes you think it was only one?"

Thinking of the prints and the blood she'd found, she answered decisively, "Evidence, my dear doctor, hard evidence."

The ease with which Dr. Whitman carried Rose upstairs surprised her. Obviously, there was more to him than met the casual eye. She wrapped her hand around his bicep and squeezed. "Hmm. I would not have taken you for a modern man who engages in daily aerobics."

"Maybe I'm simply in the habit of carrying my patients." The doctor turned sideways to manage the doorway to her study without striking her ankle against the doorframe. "Now where would you like to be deposited?" He gave a quick glance about the room. "Looks like the repairs are moving a little slow."

"The handyman we once employed has become a cowboy." She waved to her favorite overstuffed armchair. "There in the corner by the stove, please."

He didn't even grunt when he positioned her in the chair. "Would you push that footstool closer, please? Thank you." He lifted her leg, gently propping her foot atop the stool.

"Does that feel better?" he asked with genuine concern.

"Hmm." She considered feigning a need for another massage, but her pride refused the temptation.

The doctor perched on the lab stool where he could study the case points written on the chalkboard. "Should I fill in some blanks?"

"That would be helpful."

"Not until you've had some nourishment!" Mrs. Pennyworth entered the study carrying a tray of sandwiches, nearly dropping it when Sergeant brushed against her as he trotted in behind her. She huffed her disapproval. "That dog is always underfoot. Stays in the kitchen more than with his mistress."

Dr. Whitman relieved her of the tray and laid it on a cleared section of the lab table. "You are the keeper of the cupboard, Mrs. Pennyworth, and as such, greatly to be adored, dare I say worshipped, by both beast and man."

"I hardly feel either with this mutt growling at me most of the day. I never know if he's hungry or wants me to let him out. He always wants something from me."

"It's his way of communicating. He likes you," Rose said reasonably.

Mrs. Pennyworth shook her finger at Rose. "I expect you to eat a good hearty meal. Build up your strength. Doctor says so. For heaven only knows what you might do to yourself tomorrow."

Rose looked at her housekeeper with affection. "What would I do without you, Mrs. Pennyworth?"

Mrs. Pennyworth scowled at Rose and wagged her finger at the doctor. "I'm counting on you to keep her from blowing herself up again."

The doctor nodded solemnly. "I shall endeavor to make it so."

Dr. Whitman lifted the tray and took a long sniff at the stack of sandwiches. "Your Mrs. Pennyworth is a jewel." He crossed the room and offered one to Rose. "You're lucky she tolerates your reckless behavior."

"I am not reckless. My risks are all calculated. Besides, we have made no great scientific advance without risk. Taking risks is simply not the same as recklessness." Rose sniffed at his characterization and selected a cucumber sandwich. "You wouldn't call Thomas Edison reckless, would you? Our modern world is powered by experiments that involved a great number of risks."

The doctor chewed thoughtfully before answering. "You're right. But might I suggest you are less like Mr. Edison and more like Nikola Tesla, who burned down his New York lab five years ago."

"Yes, and look at what he's working on now! Have you seen the reports of his research in the use of radiation to see through flesh? Imagine the benefits to your own profession, doctor! Recognizing tumors and inflamed organs. Why, you might have discovered my ankle is indeed broken."

"Touché, my friend. But what a pity, too. You would not have had such personal attention if such was true. We physicians would become little more than mechanics, flipping switches on machines. Might I suggest that a machine would not have given your ankle such a gentle massage."

Rose scowled and plucked a cucumber from between the layers of bread.

"But I don't wish to argue with you." The doctor picked an apple from the tray and strode to the chalkboard. "Tell me about this Miss Lillian Finnegan you pursued today."

"I'm not sure what her involvement is. But innocent people do not make it a habit of fleeing in order to avoid interrogation. Wouldn't you agree?"

"A logical assumption, yes. But she might have run for reasons other than to evade your questions," he countered.

Rose pointed her sandwich at the board. "Possibly, yes. But there were two fingerprints on the windowsill made with the intruder's blood."

"Hmm. Cut themselves entering?" The doctor made a new category in chalk, **Evidence**, and wrote beneath it, **Fingerprints on windowsill**.

"Undoubtedly."

"Do you think this was only one intruder's prints."

"I do, but I have begun to think *he* may have been a *she*."

The doctor arched an eyebrow. "She? Really? What makes you think so?"

"The prints. Too small for a man."

"Could have been a youth," he conjectured.

"Yes, but the footprints outside the window bore the marks of a heel more likely made by a woman's boot."

"Ah! You didn't mention the footprint. That's not fair. You didn't share all your clues."

Rose ignored his objection and continued. "But that puts the likelihood of our Miss Lillian Finnegan as the intruder nearly out of the equation, doesn't it? Why would the woman enter through a window when she already had access from within? No, someone else, another woman, entered through the window."

Rolling the chalk in his fingers, the doctor squinted at her with a distinct look of skepticism. "You say they took nothing from the home?"

"Nothing they have as yet discovered."

Dr. Whitman studied the neat rows written in chalk. "Two break-ins. Two different methods of entry. Two different intruders."

"No motive, except for what we assume to be a vase of questionable worth."

"So, what will you do next, apart from waiting for Detective Donahue to locate your fleet-footed Miss Finnegan?"

"I want to interview the company conducting the auction for Mr. Larson's household goods. Perhaps someone there might have a better idea of the vase's worth."

Under the chalk word, **Motives**, Dr. Whitman drew a fair representation of a Greek vase, complete with small handles, then inscribed a dollar sign and a question mark next to it.

"Not a bad representation, Dr. Whitman." Rose lay her half-eaten sandwich on the plate. "The bloody prints on the windowsill should offer more insight than they do." Hitting her fist against the arm of the chair, she scowled and said, "I was born into the wrong century! If we were conducting this investigation ten or twenty years from now, think of the forensic research that might assist us? Surely, within the next few decades, physicians will know far more about identifying people from what they find in their blood."

The doctor crossed the room to collapse into the wing chair beside her. "I suppose you're referring to the article I showed you a few months ago? The Austrian physician who's working to identify types of blood?"

"Karl Landsteiner, yes." Rose leaned forward, gingerly lifting her foot to a more comfortable position. "With a sample of a suspect's blood, we might place him at a crime scene if he were injured in a struggle, or as in this case, cutting himself or herself upon entry..."

Dr. Whitman said, "I rather think Dr. Landsteiner is looking into ways his discoveries might assist the healing of patients rather than solving their deaths."

"I'm sure. But each new scientific discovery can unlock secrets to the next." She moved her foot to the floor and attempted to stand.

"Wait, let me help you."

Rose accepted his help, leaning on his arm. "Tomorrow, I'll retrieve my bag from Mrs. VanderHelm's house and try to lift a facsimile of the fingerprints." She recalled the housekeeper's exceptional regard for a spotless house. "If, that is, the obsessively fastidious Mrs. Haycraft hasn't scrubbed them away."

"I hope you'll remember that the last time you tried to use fingerprints to prove a man had been at the crime scene, they laughed you out of the courtroom."

"Yes, I remember. The time has not yet come for my vindication in that regard. But this time, it is to satisfy my own need to know."

THE CASE OF THE PECULIAR INHERITANCE

The doctor bent his head close to hers. "I'm glad you remembered. The last time I learned more about the vivid color of your vocabulary than I would have liked."

"Mark my words, Dr. Whitman, one day our judicial system will catch up to the French and admit fingerprints as proof."

He supported her arm as she limped across the room. "I can see the benefit, just so long as we don't catch up to their method of using the guillotine for executions."

"If a criminal knew he might be in jeopardy of losing his head, we might expect fewer crimes if, as a practice, we were to sever the head of the snake."

Dr. Whitman wet his lips and blinked slowly. "My dear Miss Rose, I believe Mrs. Pennyworth is correct in saying that at times your thoughts run to the macabre. If I were not an honest man and on the correct side of the law, you would terrify me."

CHAPTER 8

Dr. Whitman arrived the next morning as Rose pushed back from her bountiful breakfast. He came bearing a gift of crutches.

"I'm not sure I need these. My ankle is much better this morning, but thank you for your thoughtfulness. Surely, my recovery will not necessitate their use."

"It's wise to keep off your foot as much as possible for a day or two. Consider it a professional precaution in the event of your need to apprehend another felon." He gave her a wicked grin. "Who knows? I might have misdiagnosed the severity of your injury and you have a fracture instead. I would be forever grieved to think I had not properly treated you."

Mrs. Pennyworth stepped into the breakfast room. "You've another visitor, Miss McKenzie. Detective Donahue came to see how you're feeling this morning. Do you want me to show him in or will you meet him in the parlor?"

"I'll come to the sitting room. It will give me an opportunity to try out the crutches Dr. Whitman has brought me."

"I have to go," Dr. Whitman said. "And you have important

business to discuss. Try to stay off that ankle until it heals properly."

"As much as possible, I will follow your wise advice, doctor."

The detective waited inside the sitting room, clutching his cap in two hands. At first sight of Rose, his face brightened, but as Dr. Whitman appeared behind her, he assumed the austere demeanor of his profession.

"Detective Donahue, you know Dr. Whitman, don't you?" Rose asked.

The doctor offered his hand to the officer and stepped to the side of Rose. "Yes, good morning, detective."

The two men shook and stepped apart, forming an obtuse triangle with Rose in the position of the greatest degree of angle.

"I understand you rescued Miss McKenzie last night," the doctor said.

"I was glad to be of service." The detective's eyes tracked the crutch from beneath her arm to the hemline of her skirt. "How are you this morning? No permanent damage, I hope."

"Much improved after a night's rest and a bit of ice. I expect to be walking normally by tomorrow." She glanced over at the doctor's arched eyebrow. "If I don't overwork it today."

"That's good news. You could have been more seriously injured. I've seen a few that tangled with streetcars and it didn't turn out as well for them."

Rose said, "In all honesty, my buttocks took the worst of the blow. More shades of purple than I thought were in the color spectrum."

The detective's freckles turned a shade of scarlet.

Dr. Whitman brought his hand to his mouth and coughed. He took a step back and cleared his throat before rushing to say, "Well, I must be on my way. Appointments this morning." He looked once more at the detective, who appeared to have made some recovery. "It was good to see you again. Keep up the outstanding work of making the city safer for our fair maidens."

As soon as the doctor left the room, Rose asked the detective, "Did you locate Lillian?"

Detective Donahue squared his shoulders and nodded. "The house isn't far from where you had your accident." He gave an uncertain smile. "You were practically at her door."

"Did you learn anything about her? Has she any record of criminal activity?" Rose suggested the man take a seat.

Halfway to a sitting position, he shot upright again, a look of renewed embarrassment on his face, "I couldn't sit while you're . . . Oh, yes, uh, I forgot. It might be pain—"

"It's quite all right. Please, make us both feel better and have a seat. I'm fine standing as long as I don't rest my full weight on this ankle."

He lowered himself to perch on the edge of the chair, looking no more comfortable than before. "I found out a few things that might interest you, yes," he said as he pulled a small notebook from his uniform pocket. "The young lady's been convicted of petty theft, one charge of stealing from her employer—a mercantile shop on Hamilton Street. She claimed she only took what he owed her in back wages. The owner denied it and took her to court."

"Hmm. I could see how she might not want her current employer to know this. Most likely the reason she ran." Rose propped her crutches against the side table, tested her weight on the injured ankle, and winced.

"It's what I've seen often happen. They get a whiff of trouble and bolt." The detective ran a hand through his ginger hair and gave her a grin. "You saw it yesterday. That was a game attempt you made to catch her. Wish my men showed half your spunk when chasing down a suspect."

Rose frowned at his careless use of the word "spunk," employed to describe women more than men. Of course, men were brave or daring, while women had spunk or pluck. Silly words meant to belittle more than praise.

Detective Donahue failed to discern her disapproval and proceeded with his narrative. "I have one man watching the house. I thought that if you're feeling up to it, I could take you there now."

Rose tested her ankle again, frowned, and picked up the crutches. "Just let me get my bag. No reason to delay further."

Detective Donahue assisted Rose from the police wagon a few feet beyond the two-story brick house. Four separate entrances led to what Rose assumed to be separate living quarters.

"It's the one on the right with the window over the alley." The detective spoke low and tipped his head as a gesture to indicate a man in plain clothes lounging at the bottom of a steel fire ladder. "That's Johnson over there. If anyone tries to escape, he'll catch 'em." He gave her a conspiratorial grin. "That one enjoys running."

"Has he seen anyone else coming or going from the apartment?"

The detective gave a quick shake of his head. "He's only been stationed there a few hours. But, no, he hasn't seen anyone. You want me to accompany you? I mean . . ." He cast a glance at her foot. "Can you manage it?"

She considered the three stone steps leading to the first-floor apartment and rotated her ankle. It was still sensitive but improving. "No, I think I can manage well enough. I'm afraid that if she sees it's a policeman at the door, she'll not answer."

"Well, we'll be here if you need us. I'll just be over there at the corner of the building. You can cry out for assistance and I'll hear you."

Her eyes fixed on the curtained window of the apartment, and she nodded absently at the detective's assurances. She discerned a slight movement of the curtains on the first floor made by slender fingers.

Rose leaned heavily on one crutch and turned the doorbell key with her free hand. After a full minute, she tried a second time. Footsteps sounded from within, followed by muffled voices, one of them definitely female. The door opened a few inches.

"Yes?" A matronly woman's face appeared in the narrow opening.

"Hello. My name is Rose McKenzie. I would like to speak with Miss Lillian Finnegan, please. I believe she resides here, yes?"

THE CASE OF THE PECULIAR INHERITANCE

From inside came urgent whispers. A hushed conversation reinforced Rose's belief that Lillian stood on the other side of the door. When the woman reappeared, a nervous smile tremored across her lips. "She's not here at present. I'll tell her you called." Before the door closed, it met with Rose's crutch.

"What's this?" The woman's voice became sharp as she tried unsuccessfully to push the crutch away. "I told you she wasn't home. Please leave!"

"I think you are telling a falsehood." Lifting her voice, Rose said, "Miss Finnegan, it would be better for you to speak with me than with the detective waiting on the street behind me." Rose shifted her position enabling the older woman to have an unobstructed view of Detective Donahue. The officer touched his finger to the bill of his cap.

Her eyes widened in alarm, and the woman tugged ineffectively at the door. In the next moment, she fell back as a body shoved past her. A lanky boy charged for the front steps. Rose lifted one crutch and threw it like a javelin. The crutch entangled with the boy's legs and launched him a few feet in the air, his feet flailing.

As he landed in a heap on the sidewalk, dazed, he looked up at Rose in disbelief. He glanced back at the policeman closing in and scrambled to his feet. With a loud curse, he took off in the opposite direction.

Detective Donahue yelled over his shoulder, "Officer Johnson, we have a runner!"

Rose recovered her crutch from the steps and moved to the

sidewalk passed by the two officers in pursuit. Officer Johnson outdistanced the detective by a few yards.

Turning to look at the older woman still standing stunned in the doorway, Rose saw her raise a fist to her mouth. Rose started for the steps when again the woman gave out a startled cry. Lillian Finnegan pushed the older woman aside and tore down the steps. Only hesitating a moment at the sight of Rose blocking her way, she pulled up her skirt and leaped over the railing. In a stunning exhibition of athleticism, Lillian landed on the sidewalk with a sharp expulsion of breath. In the next moment, she jerked a bicycle from beneath the steps. In one admirably practiced move, she again lifted her skirts and swung her leg over the frame.

Rose refused to allow the young woman to evade her again. Now practiced herself, Rose took careful aim and threw the crutch. With Olympic precision, the crutch skewered the front spokes, sending Lillian into a graceful arc over the handlebars. She landed with less grace and an "oof" as the bicycle completed its arc, sans rider.

The young woman groaned and with spunk that would have impressed the detective, she stumbled to her feet.

Rose recalled the words of the Italian who'd cursed her yesterday, and she spit out the curse in perfect imitation as Lillian took off limping. Rose retrieved her scuffed crutch, and placing it once more under her arm, she resumed the chase.

Considering the woman's fall, Rose assumed she'd scarcely stand, let alone run. She should have broken her neck. But given their joint disabilities, Rose estimated a fifty/fifty chance to catch her.

It was then that Lillian glanced over her shoulder, not at Rose but at the streetcar rolling in the same direction as their slow-motion race. Surely, she wasn't considering it. Rose recalculated her chances of catching a moving streetcar. She didn't like the odds.

Lillian hobbled into the street, obviously assessing her own chance. She'd need to gauge the speed and distance to the front steps of the electric car. Lillian reached out for the hand bar, but Rose turned her attention to the back steps. Running now like a peg-leg pirate, Rose pursued the back end of the car. With the handrail mere inches from her grasp, she used the crutch to push off from the street and launch herself onto the first step. A man standing on the top landing reached down, caught her and gave her a hand up. "Must be a real important date."

Rose's icy expression cleared a path through two women blocking her view of the car's interior. She searched the backs of the passengers' heads. Maybe Lillian had changed her mind about jumping aboard. Rose bent forward to peer out a window, then scanned the passengers at the front of the car. She closed her eyes, recreating Lillian's features, her hair, her clothes.

Rose inched forward down the aisle. A few rows ahead, sitting so still as though willing herself invisible, Rose found her. Lillian must have sensed her approach because she stumbled to her feet and out into the aisle. Rose groaned. The young housemaid didn't lack for energy.

It was with a noisy explosion of breath that Lillian hit the floor.

Cries of alarm came from the women sitting on either side of the aisle when Rose dove for Lillian's legs. Before the woman could crawl away, Rose pushed herself up and planted her knee just below the woman's corset.

"I have questions for you, Miss Finnegan," Rose said breathlessly.

CHAPTER 9

Rose repositioned her foot on the chair, then sat back and picked up her teacup, sniffing at the pleasurable fragrance of bergamot. Lillian sat across from her with one leg propped in a similar fashion. The young housemaid pressed to her temple a dish towel filled with ice chips.

Lillian's words came slightly distorted by her swollen lower lip. "Where'd a fine lady like you learn to tackle like that? You must have had a tough brother growing up."

"Sister," Rose corrected before she took a sip of tea.

Mrs. Finnegan dropped the tea kettle onto the stove with a clatter. "It's her brother, Danny, that's brought all this down on our heads, him and that gang he runs with."

Lillian said, "I told you. He swore to me he quit the gang."

"Then why'd he run like that? Sure makes him look guilty." Mrs. Finnegan sagged heavily into the chair between them. "Heaven only knows what the police will do to him now."

Rose set her cup on the embroidered tablecloth and ran her finger along a curving line of stitched ivy. "The question is the same for you, Miss Finnegan. Why did you run yesterday and today? You must realize that it makes you appear complicit."

Lillian touched the dish towel to her lip and winced. Her face collapsed in defeat as she dropped her hand to the table, the ice chips scattering from the towel. Neither she nor her mother attempted to retrieve them.

"I didn't want Mrs. VanderHelm to know." She sighed and picked up a single ice chip, laying it on her trembling open palm.

"To know what, Lillian?" Rose asked.

The girl wrapped her fingers around the ice, and tears welled in her eyes.

"That they had arrested you for stealing from your last employer?" Rose asked softly.

Lillian grimaced as if Rose had struck her in the face. "Does Mrs. VanderHelm know?"

"She hasn't heard it from me."

"I didn't want to lose my job. I knew she'd not want a convicted thief working and living in her home. Then when they broke in and stole the vase and made a mess of the place, I figured the truth would come out about my record. They wouldn't have to look any further, would they?"

Rose slowly ran her finger around the rim of her teacup, noting the small chip and the hairline crack near the handle. It was canny of Mrs. Finnegan to keep an object with remaining usefulness. Such a habit might reveal something about the nature of the woman's frugality and compassion.

"Then the next night, when it happened again, I knew I had to leave. I didn't want to." She dabbed at a tear with the back of her hand. "Mrs. Haycraft is a funny old bird."

"Lillian! Don't be rude. It's not respectful."

The girl dropped her head. "Sorry. Didn't mean it so. I like her. I do. I couldn't stand to see her face when she found out …"

"But why would they suspect you? You could have remained quiet," Rose said.

"I thought about it, but then I worried about Danny."

"Why? Do you think he had anything to do with the break-in?"

"No!" She dropped her gaze to the table. "I don't think so." She glanced up. "At least I hope he didn't."

"That's not a powerful defense."

Lillian frowned. "He's been in trouble before but mostly pranks."

"Until last spring," Mrs. Finnegan added.

Lillian, her face flushed, rushed to her brother's defense. "But he denies he had anything to do with the fire in Mr. O'Reilly's shop. He swore to me on Father's grave that he didn't."

"And you almost believe him," Rose said in a kinder tone.

Lillian propped her chin in her palms and closed her eyes.

"What can you tell me about the second break-in? Mrs. Haycraft told me you heard someone downstairs. I assume you went downstairs to investigate?"

The girl sat back. From the circles beneath her eyes, Rose wondered if she'd slept in the last two days. She let out a little shuddering sigh and asked, "Mother, may I have a cup of tea?"

Mrs. Finnegan rose stiffly, looking relieved to have something purposeful to do.

"I wasn't feeling well," Lillian said in a small voice. "Worry kept me awake. I couldn't think what to do. Should I tell Mrs. VanderHelm or just quit before it all came out? Couldn't sleep with all the worry in my head. Then I heard glass breaking. You know how it sounds when glass hits the sink, like a dull clunk?

"I wondered if I'd left the window open and that old tomcat had found his way in, broke a glass or something coming through. So, I took my time on the stairs in case I could sneak up and catch him. Mrs. VanderHelm can't tolerate cats."

"I was about halfway down the stairs when I saw someone sneaking down the hall from the kitchen."

Rose said, "That's not what you told Mrs. Haycraft, is it? She told me you heard something. She didn't mention that you saw anyone."

"Thank you, Mother." Lillian sniffed at her tea and sat it back on the table before answering.

Rose inclined her head and asked, "Why didn't you tell her you saw someone, Lillian? Was it your brother?"

She met Rose's question with anger. "I told you. No. It wasn't him."

"Was it someone else you recognized?"

"He was small, like a boy."

Rose leaned forward. "Surely, you saw more than his size. You say *he*. What about hair color or clothing?"

The girl frowned. "It was dark."

"Did this person see you?"

"No. I slipped downstairs and hid behind the heavy drapes in the parlor."

"Why didn't you cry out? Weren't you frightened? There was a stranger lurking through the house. How did you know he didn't have violent intentions?"

"Because I thought it might be Danny." She dropped her gaze. "I had to be sure!"

The two Finnegan ladies took in a simultaneous breath, Lillian releasing hers first in one slow expulsion. "I was afraid he'd broken his word and gone back to that wicked crowd."

"But it wasn't your brother," Rose said.

She gave her mother an imploring look and grabbed the poor woman's trembling hand. "It wasn't, Mother. It wasn't." She turned back to Rose, shaking her head. "I should have called out then when I knew it wasn't. Don't know why I didn't. I was just kinda frozen."

"What did you observe then?"

Lillian traced the interlocking vines of the embroidery with her finger as though they might help her unravel her memories. "He was looking for something, searching closets and cupboards, but careful not to disturb things. I could see him taking his time to put things back as he'd found them. Really careful, you know? Not like the first break-in."

"Did you see him take anything?"

"Not a thing." She looked up at Rose. "That's peculiar, don't you think? I mean, Mrs. VanderHelm doesn't exactly hide her valuable silver. We wouldn't be polishing it every day if she weren't eager to show it off to visitors."

Rose pondered the observation, once again sensing she was missing the obvious. She imagined the darkened rooms and the stealthy intruder taking such extreme measures to put things back in place. "How long did you stay there watching?"

Lillian squeezed her eyes closed, appearing as though one viewing memories rolling behind her eyelids like grainy images from a Georges Méliès film. "I remember my legs feeling shaky from trying to stand so still. I worried I'd make a sound, and he'd come after me. But he finally left the parlor, and I slipped out of my hiding place and followed. I thought to duck into the open pantry, but I bumped into the table where Mrs. VanderHelm displays her best crystal vases. One almost fell over, but I caught it in time. The noise must have spooked him, 'cause he took off for the back door."

"I still can't understand why you didn't tell Mrs. VanderHelm this, especially if you'd convinced yourself that he wasn't your brother," Rose said.

"But you don't know how it is when the police have you pegged as a thief. I just knew if the police started asking questions and found out about Danny and me being brother and sister, they'd think we were working together." Tears pooled in the corners of her eyes.

Rose drained the last of her tea and lowered her foot to the ground. She looked up into Lillian's strained face and reached across the table, clasping the young woman's hand. "It's difficult when you lose trust in someone you love."

Mrs. Finnegan asked, "What will happen to my son if they catch him?"

"I assume they'll start by interrogating him. They'll see if he has an alibi and whether a witness can corroborate it." Rose tested her full weight on the afflicted ankle, then met Lillian's gaze. "But, honestly, without a crime other than breaking in and making a mess, I rather doubt they'll arrest him. Neither do I believe your employer, Mrs. VanderHelm, would press charges?"

"I suppose I should tell her everything, then."

Rose nodded. "She seems a reasonable woman. I should think you'll not forgive yourself unless you tell her."

CHAPTER 10

With Detective Donahue apparently still in pursuit of his runner, Rose required another form of transportation. She'd had sufficient excitement for the day, and the overly concerned Dr. Whitman would no doubt want her to account for her activities. In light of his impending concern, she hailed a cab rather than risk disaster on the street.

By the time she'd passed over the South Platte River bridge on her return home to the Highlands, she'd convinced herself of Lillian Finnegan's innocence. But the woman's brother, Danny, still merited her attention. His behavior required she add his name to the board of suspects. Motive remained the greatest unknown. She'd need to use her creative narrative skills to come up with some possibilities, even if they were implausible at the moment.

Mrs. Pennyworth and Sergeant met her at the door, both wearing expressions of disapproval. On the one it was an unfortunate canine genetic disadvantage, the other, a choice. The one who scowled at her asked, "You look a fright, exactly like you've been chasing down criminals again."

"Precisely. How was your morning, Mrs. Pennyworth?" Rose

skirted the imposing figure of the housekeeper, limping for the stairs.

"Where are your crutches?"

"Where I broke them, I suppose." Rose slowly ascended the stairs, calling after her, "Come, Sergeant."

Mrs. Pennyworth's voice rose an octave. "Where you broke them? What do you mean?"

"It was a necessary loss." Rose turned outside her bedroom. "May I have one of your delicious beef sandwiches? I'll be in my study reflecting on the morning's revelations." Rose judiciously avoided further interrogation by closing the bedroom door behind her.

DRESSED IN HER most comfortable linen shift and muslin gardening apron, Rose snipped the air with her pruning shears. "Mrs. Pennyworth, I'll be in the garden trimming the dahlias. If anyone should call, will you please show them the way?"

The housekeeper shot her a look of alarm. "Who are you expecting? Should I be making dinner for two? I'm not complaining. You well know that I think the doctor would make a fine catch for you."

Rose almost smiled. "I am not at all interested in playing a game of catch with men. If I ever find a man worthy of such an investment of my time and interests, it will not be because I engaged in any type of game. It will be an intellectual communion of souls and minds. The only one with whom I'll play catch is my dog, Sergeant."

As though on cue, Sergeant trotted into the kitchen and swiveled his head to give Mrs. Pennyworth a hopeful glance.

The housekeeper waved a floured hand at the dog. "I hope you're taking him with you." She shook the rag more rigorously. "That sad face won't get you anywhere with me!"

Sergeant's ears sagged even lower as an accurate measure of his disappointment. In answer to his mistress's call, he padded out the door and into the garden.

Rose meandered along the curved brick path, bordered by an extensive row of trimmed rosemary bushes. She stopped and snipped a few sprigs from the far side of the hedge, hoping her fastidious gardener wouldn't notice. Sergeant sniffed the hedge and raised a leg of salute. "That's precisely why I take my cutting from the top," she told him.

Hiding her neighbors' looming, three-story house were two plum trees that gave her particular delight in spring with their profusion of white flowers. Now, in autumn, they provided a pleasantly cooling canopy of glorious purple foliage. As she passed beneath them, she reached up, brushing her fingers along the low-hanging branches.

The path spiraled into beds of roses, a riot of colors and textures, thorns and beauty melding in natural harmony. Sergeant squeezed between her skirt and a fragrant cabbage rose heavy with white blooms. A shower of petals cascaded onto the path and Sergeant's coat. The hound circled twice, then made himself comfortable on the only patch of grass in the center of the garden.

THE CASE OF THE PECULIAR INHERITANCE

Rose closed her eyes for a full minute, pushing aside the morning's activity, the interrogation, and the empty black spaces on her chalkboard case wall. She breathed deeply of this, her haven of serenity. "A fragrance of heaven."

Sergeant responded by rolling over and fanning his oversized paws in the air, giving out a resonant howl from deep in his chest.

Focused on removing the petals from a brilliant ruby rose, she was surprised to hear her name called from a short distance away. Footsteps on the other side of the privet hedge followed the call, and bobbing along on the opposite side she saw the familiar profile of a police officer's cap. "Detective Donahue, is that you?"

The cap elevated a few inches, and the detective's eyes peered at her from under the bill of his cap. "Yes, Miss McKenzie. It's me."

"Are you lost?"

The detective looked at the path and then back at her. "Just follow the way I'm going, I suppose?"

"Yes, I'm sure you can find your way." Rose lay her basket on the stone bench beside the sleeping Basset Hound and waited. "There you are. I'm glad to see you survived your vigorous pursuit of Daniel Finnegan."

"That was quite a throw. The way you took down the boy with your crutch makes me think we should bring you onto our station's baseball team as a ringer. Saw nothing quite like it."

The detective removed his hat. Rose noticed drops of sweat on his brow and recalled the reason she'd changed into her linen shift. She took pity on the poor man looking thoroughly miserable in his woolen coat and patted the space beside her on the bench. "Please, have a seat. I can ask Mrs. Pennyworth to bring some cool lemonade."

"Already done it." Mrs. Pennyworth appeared around the hedge with a pitcher and two glasses. She gave the officer a curious Cheshire-like smile and set the tray on the stone table.

"Mrs. Pennyworth, you are a marvel. Thank you." Rose immediately filled a glass and offered it to the officer.

"I brought you something for the dog, too." The housekeeper tossed her a small ball. Her brows lifted with intentional significance and she rolled her eyes in the officer's direction. "In case you wanted to play catch."

Rose took the ball and jammed it into her apron pocket, giving the housekeeper a curt acknowledgment. "Thank you."

When Mrs. Pennyworth left them, Rose noted the officer had already drained his glass. She refilled it without asking him if he desired more and poured a glass for herself. "The fall days have turned unusually warm, haven't they?"

Detective Donahue finished his second glass and swiped the back of his hand across his lips. "Yes, they have."

"I hope you have some information for me."

"I do. We caught up with the boy or rather Johnson did."

Rose sipped at her lemonade and asked, "That's good news, and I assume you interrogated him?"

"The boy claims he and his girlfriend were with a priest at St. Andrews Church that evening. He swears he had nothing to do with the break-ins. Said that his visit to the priest was to confess some of his unsavory activities last spring and ask forgiveness." The detective pulled out his tattered notebook, glancing through it before adding, "His girlfriend threatened to break their courtship if he didn't mend his ways."

"That may be well and good, but it's not an alibi for the entire night, is it?" Rose took another sip and set her glass back on the tray. "What does your police officer's instinct tell you? Do you believe his earnest claim to innocence for the love of a woman?"

Detective Donahue's lips twitched in amusement. "My instinct tells me he's scared. It also suggests he may have operated outside the law for more incidents than we have on our books. But I can't for the life of me think why he'd risk going back to jail for a break-in like this one."

"I don't believe he had anything to do with the first. I'm uncertain of the second, but I agree the vase appears a poor motive."

"Why break in a second time if they'd already taken the vase?"

"Unless there were two different intruders, the second not realizing the vase was already stolen," Rose said.

"That's what you think? There were two different intruders?"

"Quite sure. The first involved someone knowledgeable with lock picking. The second, an amateur. I found fingerprints from a small hand on the windowsill."

The detective frowned. "You're aware Mrs. VanderHelm didn't call us in on the second one? I only learned about it from you. Guess she's taken us off the case."

"I have a feeling it wasn't your decision to refuse to investigate the first break-in." Rose studied his reaction.

The man looked down at the glass still in his hand. "I really can't say, but I can say that the captain and I don't always agree on procedure."

"But you have said. That's precisely what I assumed from your willingness to assist me."

The detective held out his glass. "May I have another glass, please?"

She obliged his request and waited for him to tell her what she believed he'd really come to say.

He emptied the third glass, then set it beside hers on the tray. "There's something that we're not seeing. It has less to do with the vase as it does with the man who sent it."

"Raymond Larson," Rose said.

"Yes. Larson was a dangerous man. He had his fingers in a lot of dirty pies. I want to know why he sent anything to a woman like Mrs. VanderHelm, who for all outward appearances never operated outside the law. She's squeaky clean from all I can determine."

His forehead creased, and he lowered his voice. "Miss McKenzie, be cautious of who you talk to and how you phrase every question. There were several wicked men who worked for and around Mr. Larson. No matter who we caught, or how hard we pressed them to implicate him, not one would. We suspected him of countless crimes in this city, but he never went to jail for anything." His voice grew more serious. "I know I can't stop you from pursuing the investigation, Miss McKenzie. But please be careful. You won't know who to trust, including those sworn to uphold the law."

CHAPTER 11

Rose leaned in close to the mirror, pushing her hair away from her forehead where the skin beneath the doctor's neat stitches remained a brighter pink. "It is because of my vanity, I suppose, that I hope for a scar. Even a small one like the doctor's would do. Don't you agree?"

Sergeant declined an opinion and lay his head atop his folded paws.

As was the fickle nature of Colorado weather, the pleasant warmth of yesterday's afternoon had departed with sunset. Autumn's chill blew across the front range at the break of day. But Rose had grown weary of her summer frocks, so she welcomed the change. Today, she donned her periwinkle-blue tweed jacket, matching straight skirt, and an ecru blouse with a touch of lace, a flattering frame for her long neck.

"Do you approve?" Rose squatted down beside the dog and stroked his silky ears. "I wish I could take you with me, but this is business, and with the strange twist this case has taken, I think you should stay and look after Mrs. Pennyworth." She lifted his chin in the palm of her hand. "Even if the detective is correct, and I can't trust anyone, I know I can depend on my Sergeant."

The mustard plasters Mrs. Pennyworth had applied to her ankle last night had worked surprisingly well, so she found the descent of the staircase far easier than the previous day. This discovery lifted Rose's spirits.

In the entry hall, she pulled on her gloves and called out to her housekeeper. "Mrs. Pennyworth, I'm going out this morning for a meeting with Mrs. Miller from Mr. Kent's office. Can you please send the boy a message to walk Sergeant again this morning?"

The housekeeper answered from a distance . . . something about, "more than he's worth."

"Please take any phone calls with sharp attention to details." Rose emphasized the last word. "Thank you! I should be home by early afternoon."

A crisp wind nearly ripped the door from her grasp as she stepped into the bright Colorado sunshine. She clapped her hand atop her hat and yanked the door closed behind her.

On a day such as this, it would have been exhilarating to ride her bicycle downtown. It was a shame it came to such a tragic end. She looked at the twisted frame, leaning like a drunken miner against the porch railing where Detective Donahue had returned it. It scarcely resembled any mode of transportation. She tilted her head, viewing it from an angle. Perhaps she could use it as a garden sculpture. The jasmine vine needed a bit of support. Maybe her gardener could devise a way to use it.

Her spirits lifted another degree, and she took the steps cautiously, working to do so without limping. A cab would have to suffice this morning.

Rose often found her height an advantage, one of which was giving her the ability to catch the attention of a cabbie. She waved at the very next one, gratified to see the man quickly direct his sleek dappled horse to the curb.

The cabbie jumped from his seat, landing with a thud on the sidewalk. "Where to, Miss?"

"The Brown Palace, please."

He offered her his hand, tipped his hat, and almost purred, "I should have guessed as much. A fine establishment for a fine lady."

Rose ignored the obvious flattery, simply smiling.

When the Brown Palace Hotel opened in 1892, Rose and Casey had been two of its earliest guests. After moving from the more established and culturally advanced city of Chicago, the sisters were delighted to discover within its unusual triangular-shaped Colorado-red stone walls the elegance more familiar in the East than in the heart of the Wild West. The architects designed the interior as a stunning display of opulence in the Italian Renaissance style.

Rose requested a table in the center of the tearoom, which afforded a full view of the eight-story, stained-glass atrium. Unarguably, it remained one of the hotel's most notable features. The lobby's tiered balconies and ornate marble walls always tickled her imagination and spurred her hope for Denver's place of distinction in the century ahead. Here, anything became possible, and a woman with purpose and determination could make a place for herself as well.

"I'm sorry I'm late."

Rose turned at the sound of the female voice and looked up into the pinched face of Victoria Miller. She immediately sensed the need to soothe the woman's distress. "Not to worry, Mrs. Miller. Please, have a seat."

The younger woman smiled in relief and thanked the waiter who held out her chair.

"I'm so glad you could take the time to join me." Rose poured the Brown Palace's signature tea into Mrs. Miller's teacup. "Sugar and cream?"

Mrs. Miller pulled off her gloves and folded them in her lap. "Oh, no thank you. I like to taste the tea."

"I couldn't agree more. I find anything additional alters the fragrance as well." Rose lifted her cup and breathed in. "I believe the scent of bergamot is absolutely restorative to the nerves."

Rose knew from experience the need to put at ease anyone she wished to interrogate. From the pinched expression the younger woman wore like hastily applied makeup, she had her work cut out for her. "We may have a few things in common. Mr. Kent told me your father is an attorney. My father was a lawyer as well. In fact, I considered studying law and following in my father's footsteps."

"What changed your mind?"

"Several unforeseen circumstances," Rose said without

elaboration. "But I remain keenly concerned with bringing the guilty to account for their crimes. I'm content with what I've chosen to do with my life."

A thin line formed between Mrs. Miller's curved brows. "Few women can make that claim, and those that do, I doubt, are being honest with themselves."

Rose settled her own cup in its saucer and searched the young woman's face. "In terms of their duties as wives and mothers?"

The young woman dropped her gaze to the linen tablecloth. "Content with their choices, I suppose. Plenty of women find fulfillment in traditional roles. Others do not, and some of them view themselves as somehow flawed not to be at peace in those duties. Some suggest that they are denying their ordained duty. But as opportunities increase for women, they may not wish to choose. They may desire to fulfill both roles."

Rose nodded in understanding. "To find a man comfortable with such a forward-thinking woman is rare indeed, but a treasure if found, no less valuable than the gold that brought so many to this part of the country."

Mrs. Miller's lips curved into a tremulous smile. "I knew such a treasure, one who did not share the predominant opinion of his gender. I actually married him." While her smile was genuine, a touch of sadness shadowed her eyes.

Rose watched the woman's lips tighten again. "You're very young to have suffered such a loss."

Mrs. Miller nodded. "We met at the university, where we took the same class in criminal law. We knew we were too much in love to wait until graduation, so with my father's reluctant blessing, we wed. My husband died a year later."

"I'm so sorry." Rose said sympathetically.

The waiter's return with a three-tiered tray of tea sandwiches and scones necessitated a pause in their conversation.

"The hotel's scones are as wonderful as I remember," Mrs. Miller said after she'd taken her first bite of biscuit generously topped with clotted cream. "My father brought me here for my eighteenth birthday. It was a magical day. Have you seen the lobby at Christmas?"

Rose nodded, remembering her first Christmas in Denver when their uncle came for a visit. She knew how much her uncle's attitude toward women in law enforcement had influenced the futures of both her and her sister. "You spoke of women presenting a threat to men by choosing to explore jobs where they can use their gifts in new, exciting ways. Although that may be true for some men, I believe it is not for all. Just as there are forward-thinking women, there are equally forward-thinking men. I firmly believe that a man who is secure in who he is can accept a woman for who she knows herself to be."

Mrs. Miller smiled and said, "I see we are in complete agreement."

Again, the waiter cut short their discussion, replacing the empty teapot with a full one. For a time, the two women indulged themselves in the epicurean delights offered by the Brown Palace. Their conversation differed little from those of other women dining around them.

Rose sat back and dabbed at the corner of her mouth with her napkin. "I do not dare to come here more often than an annual visit. I fear overindulgence on my part."

In consideration to Mrs. Miller's agitation, Rose took a more direct approach before she found an excuse to leave. "What type of law does your father practice?"

"He was a prosecutor for the state." She reached for the teapot, offering to pour a cup for Rose.

"Was? Does he not practice now?"

She took her time responding, stirring her tea as though such a simple question merited thought. At last, she said, "He became too ill to practice."

"I see."

Mrs. Miller's head came up, a spark of passion in her eyes. "He was an excellent trial lawyer. He even lectured at the university to fourth-year students on criminal law."

Rose heard pride in her voice but witnessed the pain. The anger, however, puzzled her. "When did you choose to pursue a career in law?"

"When Father first grew ill, I applied for admission to the University of Denver. I was one of only two women admitted. Mr. Kent gave me a rare opportunity to work in his practice. He's been generous with sharing his experience and not at all condescending as one might expect."

Rose found her comment both amusing and accurate. "He entrusted the details of Mr. Larson's estate to you, demonstrating a high degree of faith in your abilities." Memories surfaced of her father's difficulties with ambitious young lawyers and added, "He must have equal confidence in your integrity, too. Mr. Larson's estate appears to have been sizeable."

With another interruption from the attentive waiter, their conversation drifted to lighter subjects. It was then that the sole occupant of a nearby table came to Rose's attention. A sandy-haired man with a neck that strained the collar of his shirt sat with his back to their table, an open book in his large, rough hands. He left her with the impression of a thorn among the roses. Rose frowned and realized her conversation with the younger woman was lagging. She risked losing her opportunity to ask one more nagging question. "I'm still curious about the letter that arrived at Mrs. VanderHelm's home a full day after the package. Wouldn't it be your firm's practice to announce the bequeathing of a gift prior to delivery of it?"

Mrs. Miller touched her napkin to her lips and met Rose's eyes with a smile. "I suspect it was an oversight of an inexperienced clerk." She laughed lightly. "I hope it's the worst of the mistakes I made with Mr. Larson's estate. There were opportunities for several errors."

The waiter bustled up to the table again, this time with the check on a silver tray. He glanced at Mrs. Miller and said, "If there is nothing more I can do for you ladies, I wish you a pleasant afternoon and hope we see you again soon here at the Palace." Rose thought his smile was a little more suggestive than was appropriate but took the bill from the plate and thanked him.

At the table next to them, the man sat stiffly, the open book still in his hands. For all his apparent fascination with it, she'd swear he never once turned a page since she'd first noticed him.

Rose stepped out into the bright sunlight and lifted a hand to shield her eyes. The other she offered to Mrs. Miller. "Thank you for meeting with me. I enjoyed our visit. Perhaps we can luncheon again sometime."

"Thank you. I enjoyed our talk as well." She held Rose's hand with a fair grip, and she appeared on the verge of saying something more. Two gentlemen in rough western attire emerged from the hotel at that moment, lifting their hats to the two women and forcing Rose to step aside for them to pass.

The moment passed and Mrs. Miller tucked her bag beneath her arm. "I must be going. Mr. Kent said he could spare me for only an hour."

Rose called out to her. "You still have my card?"

The younger woman nodded, waved, and hurried off down Tremont Street.

Rose watched her go, realizing the truth in what she'd told the woman earlier. They had something in common—a father to whom they were devoted and a shared passion for justice.

CHAPTER 12

The blue-and-white sign bolted above the warehouse door bore the name MCALLISTER AND SONS in large block letters. Rose noticed they had mounted it crooked by at least two inches. Whether it reflected poorly on the McAllisters or their sign maker, she didn't know. Whoever was to blame, the misalignment made a poor statement for the company's work and attention to detail.

A flat-faced man with a clipboard wedged between his broad forearm and even broader chest approached her as she entered the cluttered front office. "May I help you, Miss?"

"I have some questions about the Raymond Larson estate auction. Are you Mr. McAllister?" Rose offered her hand. The young man stared at her gloved hand a moment as though considering how to label and price it. After reaching a conclusion, he clasped her hand in his burly one and shook it once. "One of them."

"A son, you mean?"

"Yep. Father doesn't do much with the hands-on work these days. What do you want to know about the Larson auction? It's not until next Thursday, and I can't sell anything in advance." He said this last somewhat mechanically, as though he'd encountered such requests with some frequency.

"I have no interest in purchasing anything. I just have a few questions."

"Shoot." His sour expression relaxed and he glanced around at the clutter, then picked up a stack of ledger books from what appeared to be a Chippendale dining chair with claw and ball feet. If not for the formidable tear to the upholstered seat and the gouged front knees, it might have fetched a doorman's full annual income. He gestured with a beefy hand for her to sit. "We're still working on cataloguing it." He thumped the clipboard he'd deposited on the desk when he took his own seat.

Rose said, "I can see you're a busy man, so I'll get right to the point. Were you aware of any items set aside from those selected for auction?"

He rubbed the back of his neck, his gaze drifting over her shoulder. After a few moments of hard thinking, he leaned back in his chair and said, "There were a few, yep. Not many, considering the size of the estate." He flipped through the papers attached to his clipboard. "Kent, Charles Kent, Larson's attorney. His office contacted us over a month ago. Probably when they knew their client was dying. We weren't allowed in until the old man died, but Kent's assistant gave us a general idea of the job."

"Mrs. Miller?"

THE CASE OF THE PECULIAR INHERITANCE

"Pretty young lady, yes."

Rose noticed he didn't have to check his clipboard to recall her name. "Was she present when you first entered the house?"

"The housekeeper met us at the door, but said we couldn't come inside until Mrs. Miller got there."

"Did you think that unusual?"

"Well, not really. If the household items amount to a lot of additional value for the estate, someone, often a legal representative, is present to make sure we do things as the deceased requested. As far as gifts not intended for auction, sometimes it can be Aunt Martha's china teapot that causes a family feud and legal battles. Relatives favor certain things that have little value . . . pictures and such. Jewelry is a hotly debated one, even if it's paste."

"So, I presume you walked through the house with Mrs. Miller before your crew started removing items from the house."

"Room by room. Standard practice."

"Did you notice if he was a collector of anything? Silver or porcelain perhaps?"

"Saw nothing like that. I've seen some collections. Odd things people hang onto. Some are worth little more than the stuff they're made of." He shook his head and blew a whistle. "Some things make you wonder about people. Last year we had an estate where the lady collected wedding dresses. Yep, wedding dresses. Spooky. She had them all hung up on the walls in her attic."

"Sounds like an interesting job."

"Sometimes. Mostly, it's just work. So, what were you looking for? Sounds like you're asking about something specific."

"Yes, actually. Did you see any porcelain vases in the house? They described it to me as blue and about..." Rose held her hands the approximate length of the trunk.

"Eighteen inches, looks like." He frowned and consulted his papers again. "Nothing in the itemized list, and I remember nothing like that. But you gotta remember, this was a five-bedroom house and unless that vase was made of gold, I probably wouldn't have noticed."

His eyes narrowed slightly, giving Rose the distinct impression of how the man might appraise the value of a fine piece of furniture. "Does someone think one of my men took it?"

"Oh, not at all. I'm investigating a break-in and trying to recover something I've never seen."

"Hmm. What are you? Surely, don't look like any police I've seen. Are you one of those lady Pinkerton detectives? Must be something your client thinks is valuable if she hired a Pinkerton."

Rose ignored the question and the comment. Instead, she pulled her card from her bag and handed it to the man. "If you recall anything more, please call me." She stood and offered her hand again. This time, the man took it immediately. "Thank you. I appreciate the time."

Leaving the warehouse to flag down a cab, she reflected on what information she had gleaned. About the appearance of the vase, Mr. McCallister offered nothing to add to Mrs. VanderHelm's description of it as unattractive. If Mr. McCallister was truthful, he'd not even noticed it. That meant there remained a space on her chalkboard under the category of Motive.

Rose thought about the man at the restaurant, the one who read his book so slowly. She'd judged him based on his appearance. Sometimes people were what they appeared. Sometimes not. It could be true of the vase. Could it be more than it appeared? They'd found art masterpieces before beneath garish, amateur paintings. It was something to contemplate.

CHAPTER 13

"You broke both crutches?" Dr. Whitman's asked with scarcely a trace of remonstration.

"Yes," Rose said.

Dr. Whitman continued to stare at her with no expression she could interpret.

"Would you like some tea?" She started off for the parlor, Sergeant keeping pace behind her.

"Clara is in the buggy. I thought we were going to the park. Didn't you ask me to bring her along?" the doctor asked.

Rose spun on her heels. "This is Tuesday?"

"Yes, this is Tuesday," he answered blandly.

"You're correct. I did ask you to bring your dog." She took to the stairs, calling back over her shoulder, "I won't be a minute. Why don't you visit with Mrs. Pennyworth while I change?"

Dr. Whitman waited for her in his buggy along with Clara and a wicker picnic basket. From the way Clara's nose remained glued to its side, Rose was certain Mrs. Pennyworth had packed it with something glorious which, judging from the aromas in the house, she'd been preparing all afternoon. "What would I do without

Mrs. Pennyworth?" Rose asked as the doctor lifted Sergeant into the back seat with Clara.

"I believe it is a question we can never ask too often," Dr. Whitman said gravely.

"Sarcasm doesn't become you, Dr. Whitman." Rose lifted her skirt and stepped into the buggy, settling herself next to the doctor.

"I shall endeavor to mend my ways, Miss McKenzie." The doctor slapped the reins with utmost precision, and the gray responded by stepping out at a quick trot.

"It's certainly cramped in here with the four of us," Rose observed. "Have you thought of purchasing a larger buggy?"

"It's interesting that you should ask. Today, I spoke with a gentleman at The Felker Cycle Company—"

"Where I bought my safety cycle?" Rose asked.

"Yes. Mr. Felker has ordered ten locomobiles, shipped by freight car to Denver. He had one on display. It's steam-powered and can get up to a speed of forty miles an hour! Imagine that! That's faster than a train. Amazing."

"I was just thinking of a larger buggy, Dr. Whitman. A locomobile?" She turned to look at him. "I would have thought with your temperament and concern for safety, such an idea would not have occurred to you."

He frowned and lifted his chin in offense. "Maybe you know me less well than you think."

"Forty miles an hour." Rose imagined herself chasing after criminals in such a vehicle. Casey would never consider such a conveyance because she scorned all things modern. "When are these steam locomobiles arriving?"

"He isn't certain, but he has one on display. I sat behind the wheel. The seats are as comfortable as those one might find in a parlor. If I were to purchase one, we might accommodate Mrs. Pennyworth for an outing." The doctor changed the topic rather abruptly. "But tell me, what did you learn today? Mrs. Pennyworth told me you had lunch with Mr. Kent's assistant."

"I learned we have more in common than she even realizes," Rose said, reaching back to scratch Clara's head. "There is something that troubles me about her, something I can't put my finger on. I don't think she's being fully candid with me. She's guarded, especially concerning her father."

"What do you mean?" Dr. Whitman put up his elbow to force Clara back. "Sit down, girl. Be good like Sergeant."

"It's obvious she's devoted to him, but there's anger in her I cannot understand."

"Didn't you tell me her father was a lawyer? Here in Denver?"

Rose grabbed the side of the buggy as Dr. Whitman veered around a slow carriage. "He was. All she said was that he had to give up his practice because of his health."

The driver of the oncoming carriage blasted his horn, causing the gray to jump to the side. Clara started barking. "Hush, girl." Dr. Whitman made soothing sounds to the spooked horse, struggling to get her under control.

"Another thing I find puzzling is why a lawyer with Mr. Kent's reputation would accept a client such as Larson, who's likely involved with criminal activity. That's illogical. Why did Mr. Kent hand over the details of the estate to a law clerk? I mean, she's no doubt vastly qualified, but my father wouldn't have done that."

"Here we are." Dr. Whitman pulled up on the reins and the buggy came to a stop at the curb. "We've a wonderful dinner, thanks to your Mrs. Pennyworth. A perfect early fall evening and two spoiled dogs. What do you say we talk of anything and everything but Mrs. VanderHelm's mysterious break-in for the next two hours?"

"Let's talk about the locomobile?"

The doctor's face opened into a broad grin. "Positively. A marvelous invention with fascinating possibilities." He jumped down from the carriage and hefted the picnic basket from the back.

"Indeed," Rose said. She didn't wait for the doctor to assist her down but took the dogs' leashes in hand and waited for him on the lawn. "Can you imagine what forty miles an hour feels like? Why, I'd think such speed would require eye protection."

"What an astute suggestion, Miss McKenzie. There's much money to be made by such an industry, I should think."

"Traveling at such speeds, as you suggest, must be how it feels to fly, and that is something I intend to experience in the coming century."

Dr. Whitman released the dogs from their leashes, letting them romp off on their own. He offered his arm to Rose, and smiled. "You see? We can discuss matters other than murder and mayhem if we put our minds to it."

BEFORE ROSE HAD stepped up on the porch, the door flew open and Mrs. Pennyworth burst from the house, waving a piece of paper. "That lady from the lawyer's office called you just minutes ago. She sounded most distraught, and she asked you to come right away." She shoved the paper into Rose's hand. "Here's the address. It's not far."

Dr. Whitman no sooner wrangled both dogs from the buggy, when he called out to Rose, "Come on. I'll drive you."

"Give me the beasts," Mrs. Pennyworth said, and grabbed the leashes from the doctor.

Rose gave the housekeeper a quick kiss on the cheek. "Thank you, Mrs. Pennyworth. You are a gem."

"So you keep sayin'. Don't notice you paying me like I was." The housekeeper rolled her eyes and tugged both dogs up the steps.

CHAPTER 14

Rose jumped from the buggy while Dr. Whitman secured his gray to the hitching post outside Mrs. Miller's home. No lights were visible inside. Rose reached into her bag and pulled out the .32 Smith and Wesson.

Dr. Whitman whispered, "Do you really think that's necessary?"

Rose said flatly, "I don't know, Dr. Whitman. Do you want to walk into a darkened house from which we have just received an urgent call for help with your buggy whip? Or perhaps your medical bag would be sufficient protection."

Dr. Whitman scowled at her. "You don't have to be sarcastic."

She responded to his remark with a single lift of her eyebrow before returning her attention to the house.

"Besides, Mrs. Miller said nothing about an intruder," the doctor reminded her.

"But she said it was urgent she speak with me, and after two break-ins already, caution is prudent. Aren't you the one who tells me to reduce my risks?" Rose approached the house with her pistol gripped in two hands, her eyes taking in the house's perimeter, the alley to the side, and the high hedge lining a sidewalk leading around the house. She listened, as one afflicted with blindness.

"Should I find the back door?"

Before Rose could affirm his suggestion, a woman's voice cried out from an open upstairs window. Both the doctor and Rose ran for the front door. Locked. She couldn't take the time to pick it, but neither had anyone else. She didn't wait to explain but started off around the house, the doctor racing behind her.

The door facing the alley stood ajar where angry voices came from within.

Rose whispered over her shoulder, "I'm going in."

Dr. Whitman pushed past her, reaching the doorsteps ahead of her. "I'll go in first." Somewhere along their route he'd picked up a wicked-looking garden hoe. He was brandishing it like a club as he opened the door. Although it was superior to a buggy whip as a defensive weapon, it was no match for her Smith and Wesson.

She pushed the doctor aside and whispered, "Don't be ridiculous." Based on their past disagreements, she feared he was about to debate the definition of gallantry. But from upstairs came a sharp cry of pain. The sounds of a struggle ensued, followed seconds later by a gunshot.

Both Rose and the doctor sprinted through the kitchen in search of the stairway.

"Here!" The doctor called from the darkened hallway. He was

already on the first landing when a figure collided with him, knocking the doctor off his feet. Rose raised her pistol, but the man careened down the stairs before she could get a clear shot without the risk of shooting the doctor. The man pushed her roughly aside and staggered for the backdoor.

Rose shouted at the doctor. "You go upstairs and check on Mrs. Miller!"

The doctor might have shouted something in protest, but Rose was in pursuit and halfway to the door. She saw the man fling himself through the door and stumble down the back steps.

"Stop or I'll shoot!" For a moment, Rose wondered if her sister would announce her intentions of lethal intent to a fleeing criminal. "Stop!" She yelled again as she shot through the door behind him.

The man stumbled in ever-slowing steps but darted behind the tall hedge and into the alley. Rose closed the gap between them and rounded the hedge with her weapon raised. The next moment, a horse and rider tore past her, knocking her to the ground.

Rose scrambled to her feet and glared down the alley where the horse veered left onto the street. "Blazes!"

In an upstairs room, she found the doctor on his knees tending to Mrs. Miller, who lay still amidst the wreckage of the room. Dr. Whitman looked up as she entered. "She may have a concussion. I know she has a broken arm."

"But not shot?"

He shook his head. "No. You know, don't you, that whoever

did this wasn't just a petty thief?"

Rose nodded and said, "I'll call the police and an ambulance."

"I already did," said a man's voice behind her.

With her pistol raised, Rose turned to the frail figure standing in the doorway. She strode to his side and wrapped her arm around his shoulders. "You must be Mrs. Miller's father. My name is Rose McKenzie, and this is Dr. Whitman. We're here to help. Are you unhurt?"

"Is she all right?" The older man started for his daughter, leaning heavily against Rose for support. Seeing her lifeless body, he cried out again, his voice rising in pitch. "Is she all right?"

The doctor rose to his feet, pulled off his coat, and draped it around the older man. "She's all right. Aside from a broken arm and some bruises, she'll be okay." Dr. Whitman looked over the man's head and gave her a warning look. Apparently, the doctor felt it unwise to suggest his daughter's possible concussion. "Let's get you off your feet." Together they helped him into an armchair. "What's your name, sir?"

"Mayhew, Clarence Mayhew." He grabbed the doctor's arm. "My girl! What did they do to my girl?" He covered his face with his hands and sobbed. In a muffled voice he moaned, "I knew this would happen one day. Knew it would happen."

The physician's eyes scanned the man's face and overall condition. Aside from the shock of having his home invaded and his daughter assaulted, he appeared unharmed. The doctor patted the man's hand and glanced up at Rose with a silent appeal to take his place at the man's side.

THE CASE OF THE PECULIAR INHERITANCE

Rose knelt beside the man's chair. As much as she loathed the idea of questioning someone as upset as Mr. Mayhew, she needed to know details they'd lose in the flurry of activity, overwhelming any clear memories of what had transpired here. "Did you see the man who did this, Mr. Mayhew?"

He continued to hold his head in his hands as if he had not heard her, repeating the words, "Knew it would happen. Knew they'd come."

Rose leaned in close and asked quietly, "Mr. Mayhew, who did you know would come?"

The man was beyond reason. His wails replaced the words, and he rocked back and forth in his chair, still covering his face and weeping.

Feeling Dr. Whitman's hand on her shoulder, Rose looked up into his grim expression. "Rose, he can't hear you right now. You're only making it worse."

She frowned and rose to her feet with a heavy sigh. "Then I must see what the house can tell me."

Thoroughly ransacked, the room presented a challenge. Books torn from shelves. Drawers pulled from cabinets. Furniture upturned. Law books scattered about indicated this would have been a study, perhaps once belonging to the father.

From the careless manner of the search, she surmised whoever had done this was also the one who'd committed the first entry into Mrs. VanderHelm's home. There was evidence of the small handprints at the second entry. The man she pursued from the house had no such diminutive hands.

But there was another way in which this break-in differed from the first two. The intruder hadn't stopped with a search. Whoever it was didn't want to leave this time without what he'd come looking for.

The doctor asked, "Rose, did you see this?"

She stepped carefully over the scattered evidence to kneel beside him on the carpet. He pointed to the bright crimson drops looking like a trail of cinnamon candy through the door and into the hall. That's why he looked like a drunken man. She felt a momentary flash of irritation that the doctor had seen the evidence before she had.

"I'd say your Mrs. Miller knew he was coming." Dr. Whitman tipped his head, his gaze pointing to a pistol lying beneath the desk chair, a Colt 38. "That's not something a lady carries casually in her handbag."

Rose kneeled beside the pistol. "It's an effective weapon for home protection. Her father might have kept it in his desk. I know my father had one very similar to this, an earlier model, but equally deadly."

It hadn't helped him when he needed protection most. A heavy throbbing in her temples cued her to relax her clenched jaw. She squeezed her eyes tight and forced the memory to slide back into its dark chamber. The police would be here in minutes, and she needed to see everything before they came and trampled what might help her understand what had happened and how the puzzle pieces fit together.

"Do you need anything from me?" she asked the doctor.

THE CASE OF THE PECULIAR INHERITANCE

"I can handle this. Go! Use that memory of yours and record the scene." He gave her an encouraging nod before returning to his patients.

Her first thought was to check the point of entry—the kitchen.

As she suspected, the intruder had picked the back lock. There were prints, larger than the ones she'd seen at the second break-in. She had to assume the first two intruders were not working together. The second assumption didn't require a great leap. Whoever *they* were, they weren't after the vase.

Without the ability to question the eyewitness, she had to rely on what physical evidence remained. She did a quick sweep of the downstairs. With everything neatly in place, the intruder had only intended to search the upstairs room. So, with the imminent arrival of the police and her time limited as well, she returned to the study.

She stood in the center of the room and rotated in place, imagining the space divided into four precisely cut slices of pie and placing each piece of furniture and pile of books as set pieces on a stage. When she returned home, she'd recall each slice and pull them together like slides in a stereoscope. She snapped her eyes closed after memorizing the items in each quadrant and turned her attention to a closer examination of the room.

Rose looked around and under every object, large and small, moving clockwise around the room, until coming to the desk. Among the papers scattered there, she found evidence that Mrs. Miller currently used the desk. A stack of correspondence with the Kent return address apparently held no interest to the thief as they remained neatly piled at the far edge of the blotter.

The sound of voices and wheels on gravel brought her head up. The police had arrived, and she'd yet to find anything useful. Frustrated, she stepped back from the desk and squinted at the cluttered surface. Something didn't fit. A sheet of paper stood out from the rest. Unlike the linen stationary of the correspondences, this one was handwritten on coarse paper. She tugged it free from beneath a torn book at the corner of the desk and found two sentences on it.

> *If you use what you know, there will be consequences. I'm coming.*

Minutes later, Rose stood beside the doctor, watching as the attendants lifted Mrs. Miller into the horse-drawn ambulance. Dr. Whitman said, "I'm going to take Mr. Mayhew with me to the hospital. Do you want to come along?"

Detective Donahue stepped up between them, his face devoid of its usual good humor. "Actually, I'd like Miss McKenzie to remain a little longer. I have some questions about what brought her here tonight." He turned a steely eye on the doctor and nodded. "You go along with your patient. I'll come by later to ask you the same. If we're in luck, the lady might be awake by then."

Dr. Whitman caught Rose's eye with an unspoken request for assurance. Rose nodded. "Go on, Dr. Whitman. Perhaps the detective will be kind enough to bring me to the hospital when he's finished here."

THE CASE OF THE PECULIAR INHERITANCE

For Rose, Detective Donahue pulled up a thin smile. "I'd be happy to do so." He tipped his head toward the front door. "If you'd come with me then."

He led them through the front door and down the entry hall to the kitchen where he faced her. "I'm more than a little curious about how you are involved in three break-ins when they're the only ones we've had in these neighborhoods for months."

She didn't bother to hide her irritation, replying caustically, "Maybe because they are all connected?"

Her answer only fueled his anger as he shot back, "Then why don't you tell me how they are—connected."

"If I knew that, I would immediately solve all three and you could mark the case closed."

"What brought you here tonight?" he demanded.

"I told the other officer who incidentally asked the same question, that Mrs. Miller called my home and spoke with my housekeeper. She wanted to see me as soon as possible. She said it was urgent." A warmth crept up her neck, the result of the slow boil of resentment churning in her stomach. "Detective Donahue, are you really going to make me repeat everything I told the officer? It would be a tragic waste of your time and mine."

His lips thinned. "I'm doing my job, Miss McKenzie. There was a shooting here tonight. That's a serious business."

She studied him for an uneasy moment. "Is someone . . . Are you under pressure from your superiors?"

His eyes flickered from hers for a mere second before he squared his shoulders and said icily, "I told you, this is my job. I'm doing my job. Now, please answer my question."

She blew out a puff of frustration and accepted that the only way she was going to get to the hospital was to cooperate or at least show a semblance of cooperation. But she didn't have to like it. Neither did she have to tell him everything she *assumed* to be true.

DR. WHITMAN MET Rose at the door to his patient's room. The detective pushed past them and strode into the hospital room. "Is she awake?"

The doctor threw a puzzled look at Rose before answering. "No. The blow to her head caused considerable trauma. I'm uncertain of the extent."

The detective pulled out his notebook and asked, "What about the young lady's father? Is he coherent yet? Can I question him?"

Dr. Whitman shook his head. "I gave him a small dose of chloral to help him sleep. The medicine I saw in his bedroom indicates he has a serious heart condition. This situation is most likely putting a strain on his already fragile health."

The detective snapped his notebook shut, glanced once more at the patient, then back at Rose. He cleared his throat and looked almost apologetic before delivering his next words. "The next time you suspect the police should be involved, I expect you to call me directly. We can't have private citizens acting as representatives of law enforcement."

"You mean, if I was a Pinkerton agent, you'd allow me to

operate freely?" Rose asked bitterly.

"Yes. But you aren't, are you? Even then, there are jurisdictions to observe. This is a case for the Denver police."

Rose felt Dr. Whitman's hand on her arm before she said, "Excuse me for noticing details, but wasn't it the Denver police that refused to investigate Mrs. VanderHelm's case?"

"I told you. That wasn't my choice."

"But this is," Rose said, unable to contain the frustration from coloring her tone of voice.

Detective Donahue appealed to the doctor. "I'm trusting you to . . . remind her of what is and what isn't her responsibility."

The doctor forced his hands into his coat pockets and said calmly, "Detective, I think you misjudge my degree of influence on the lady. Miss McKenzie is an independent and forward-thinking woman. Trust me when I say she rarely heeds my suggestions."

Before Rose could say another word in protest, the detective had left the room, the door closing soundly behind him. She took a step to follow him, but the doctor reached out for her arm, effectively restraining her. Rose shook off his hand and spun to face him. "You can't imagine that I will leave that affront to go unchallenged. To speak to me as though I need handling like someone's pet! How dare he!"

She spun to the door again, but Dr. Whitman stepped between her and the door. "Rose, wait."

"Please move," she said, her temples pounding with rage.

"Rose, try to think of Donahue's position before you explode.

He's been a great help to you over the past few years. Hasn't he?"

She frowned and reached for the handle a second time. He blocked her again. "Use that intuitive brain to discern what might have altered his behavior toward you and your profession."

Stepping back, she dropped her gaze to the tiled floor, recalling with photographic clarity the detective's facial reaction when she'd asked if someone was pressuring him. That could explain it. She looked into the doctor's face, stating what she knew to be true. "Someone is displeased with him for helping me?"

"I think it's more than likely. In fact, displeasure is probably a word too mild for the pressure being placed upon him. You've said it yourself. The world of law enforcement can be a closed brotherhood, and you, my dear Miss McKenzie, will never be mistaken for anyone's brother."

CHAPTER 15

Sergeant moaned with pleasure as Rose scratched the velvet fur beneath his ponderous ears. She'd been staring at the chalkboard long enough that her tea had cooled.

Apart from her conviction that the vase was not the reason for the break-ins, she felt less sure of arriving at a solution than she had this morning. She nudged Sergeant's rump off her foot and tried to stand. "Oh my! That is not pleasant." Rose rotated her ankle first one way and then the other to bring some circulation back into her tingling foot and limped to the chalkboard.

"Pay attention, Sergeant. We can't really rule out any of the suspects, not until we find out what we're looking for. I think the note left for Victoria or her father is now our most critical piece of evidence. Remember what it said?" The Basset Hound was on his back with his ears spread out like wings. "No, you wouldn't. You weren't there." After erasing the word "vase" with the cuff of her sleeve, she picked up the chalk and wrote the message: "If you use what you know, there will be consequences. I'm coming."

"Assuming the intruder sent the message we found tonight, it's knowledge, not an object, that's being sought."

Sergeant whimpered in his sleep and flopped his paws in pursuit of some dream bunny.

"What does he think she knows?" She underlined the last three words, "what you know."

She sunk onto the stool and crossed her arms. "Unless the two cases are unrelated and the break-ins coincidentally involved intersecting subjects." She jumped to her feet and drew two intersecting circles within the largest black area of the board. "If the circle on the left represents the two break-ins at the VanderHelm house and the second circle represents the Mayhew house intrusion, then the intersection will show us who has an involvement in each house." She wrote **Mrs. VanderHelm** in the far-left circle and immediately beneath her name, **Mrs. Haycraft** and **Lillian Finnegan**. After staring at the board for a while, she added **Danny Finnegan**. Within the right circle, she wrote **Mr. Mayhew** and **Victoria Miller**.

"As far as we know, these . . .," she checked the names of VanderHelm, Haycraft, Lillian and Danny, ". . . people have no connection to Mrs. Miller or her father." She tapped the chalk against her chin. "Except for the charity event she attended with Miss Gaylord, the secretary."

"That puts Victoria Miller within the intersecting circle." She frowned and wrote Mrs. Miller's name in the center of the two circles. "But she's a victim of the third break-in."

Rose tapped the chalk against the space under the category of Motive, then felt her eye twitch, a sure sign of her frustration.

"Mr. Raymond Larson, how do you fit into any of this?" She dropped the broken chalk into a teacup and started across the room. "Sergeant, we must write!"

The dog lifted one ear at her voice and shook his head, sending both ears swinging. He stretched, then padded after his mistress into the room behind the bookcase.

"You look like a rooster with his tail to the wind." Mrs. Pennyworth sat a plate of biscuits dripping with sausage before Rose. "Up late again, I suppose."

"Mrs. Pennyworth, you know I could not do half so well without you, but I would appreciate it if you would not make your pronouncements about my appearance such a regular morning salutation. Just once, it would be so nice to hear a sunny, 'Good Morning, Miss Rose,' or, 'It's a lovely morning, Miss Rose.'"

Mrs. Pennyworth picked up the teapot and gave her a syrupy smile. "Good morning, Miss Rose. It's a lovely morning. You still look like a rooster with his tail to the wind." She poured the tea into Rose's teacup and left the room.

"What would I do without you, Mrs. Pennyworth," Rose muttered.

She'd taken only a single bite of biscuit when Mrs. Pennyworth reentered the breakfast room with Dr. Whitman following behind. "The doctor will be honest with you. She looks frightful, doesn't she? Stayed up half the night."

"I did not stay up half the night."

Mrs. Pennyworth rolled her eyes and set another place across from Rose. "Good to see you, doctor. Lovely morning isn't it?" she asked in a tone as light as springtime air.

"Indeed, it is, Mrs. Pennyworth."

"Would you care for some eggs and biscuits?"

"Just coffee, if you have some. Unfortunately, I already had my breakfast. Thank you."

Mrs. Pennyworth bustled through the door, calling back, "I'll bring a pot right out."

Rose looked glumly at the doctor. "Why doesn't she greet me like that? All I ever get is a critical review of my appearance." She stabbed a piece of sausage.

"You don't look your freshest."

"Mrs. Pennyworth compares me to poultry and you refer to my appearance as if I was produce from the market. Let's change the subject. What's the news from the hospital? I assume you've made your rounds already or you wouldn't be here." He had circles beneath his eyes and a tight line of his normally soft lips. "You don't look so good yourself."

Mrs. Pennyworth flounced through the door with a cup and a pot of coffee. "Here you go, doctor. Hope it's strong enough for you. Know you like it with legs."

"Thank you, Mrs. Pennyworth. It smells wonderful."

She left them again and Rose asked, "Were you with Mrs. Miller?"

He poured a spoonful of sugar into his coffee, taking his time to answer. "I checked in on her frequently, but I spent time with her father, as well. I convinced him to stay in the room with her where I could monitor them both."

"There's something else on your mind. You look troubled. Are you worried she won't recover?"

He shook his head and lifted the cup to his lips, then setting it down before taking a sip. "I'm worried about you, if you care to know."

Rose sat back. "Me? Why?"

"This isn't a simple robbery anymore, Rose."

Rose opened her mouth to respond, but the doctor held up his hand to stop her. "I know you refuse to answer to anyone. I also know you can shoot a gun better than anyone I've observed. You're quick. You're clever. You're resourceful."

"Excessive flattery, Dr. Whitman, elicits suspicion."

"Don't joke about this. A woman is in the hospital. I saw the note, just like you. *There will be consequences*. If you go much further with your investigation, you'll know whatever it is you shouldn't know. Then you'll be a target in range of the consequences."

"Mrs. Miller was the one with the gun, not the intruder," Rose reminded him.

"What did that do for her? She may have permanent brain damage because of having her head bashed in."

"That's a bit melodramatic for you."

"All right. Bashed in isn't an actual medical term."

"Dr. Whitman ... Taylor ... I appreciate your concern, but I know what I'm doing. I'm not intentionally taking foolish risks. Didn't I take you with me last night?"

"A lot of good I did you. Who carried the gun and chased the man into the alley?"

"You were my backup." Rose suddenly had the amusing impression that her dog, not Dr. Whitman, sat across the table from her, looking at her with his mournful eyes.

"You aren't taking my concerns seriously."

She dropped her eyes to her plate and cut off a slice of biscuit, trying to shake the image. "I am. I really am."

"No, I don't think you are. You know, I have a great affection for you, Rose. I'm fearful that a day will come when I'll not be able to heal your injuries with a few stitches or a cold compress."

Rose observed the doctor's pinched features and felt somewhat remorseful for her lack of sensitivity. She started with a gentler tone, wanting to make amends. "I appreciate what you're saying. I do. But I believe that I'm proceeding with all due caution. I won't—"

Before she could finish, Mrs. Pennyworth hurried into the room. "Dr. Whitman, a nurse from the hospital, just called. She'd like to speak with you right away."

The doctor threw down his napkin and strode from the room.

Mrs. Pennyworth remained in the room, her hands now planted on her hips, eyes barely more than slits.

"Yes, Mrs. Pennyworth?"

"You should listen to the doctor."

"I often do, Mrs. Pennyworth."

"You more often don't."

"Does this have anything to do with our previous baseball conversation concerning the art of catching?"

She looked confused. "I'm referring to the doctor warning you about getting yourself mixed up in things the police should be handling."

"Cases involving lost dogs are acceptable, I suppose?" Rose said ruefully.

Dr. Whitman returned to the breakfast room, his serious physician demeanor in place, which made him look older than she knew him to be. "I'm sorry, ladies. I have to go."

"Is it Mrs. Miller?" Rose asked, as she quickly calculated the time it would take her to change her attire.

"No, another patient." He picked up his coffee cup from the table and took a long drink. After setting the cup on the table in an exaggerated effort of care, he looked up, holding her eyes with his. "This conversation isn't over."

Rose sighed and dropped her chin into her palm. "No, you're right. I think Mrs. Pennyworth is desirous of continuing it for you." To herself she mumbled, "I should have stayed in bed."

CHAPTER 16

Dear Casey,

Received your telegram this morning. After a breakfast that didn't settle well in my stomach, I found your message of a successful arrest a relief from the downward curve my day took this morning. Had I been in Colorado Springs to celebrate with you, I'd have treated you to dinner. We could have ordered champagne and since neither of us can tolerate it, you might have bathed in it. Of course, that would scandalize Mrs. Pennyworth. I must confess I take a wicked delight in that from time to time, especially when she voices her opinions with such persistence.

Today, I could benefit from your eye to details. Since the two men I thought to be forward-thinking individuals have independently concluded that I am too frail of body to protect myself, I am abandoned to resolve this case alone. This happens just as I sense I am on the cusp of discovering critical information.

Nearly every suspect thus far has either a plausible alibi or no obvious motive. It is the motive that has continued to escape me. Until last night, that is. If I am to follow my instincts and assume the break-in that occurred at a separate residence is connected to the first two, then it is information or a document with information that is the motivation. This changes the entire direction of my investigation. It also places on the chess board new players. More importantly, the threatening note left at the scene provides a suggestion of motive.

As far as hard evidence, I have only the wooden doll chest in which they delivered the stolen item. I can see it now from where I sit, so like the two that Mother gave us as children. When I opened the lid, I half-expected to see my dear Caroline sleeping inside. Remember all the adventures our two dolls had? By the way, I still haven't forgiven you for cutting Caroline's curls. Unlike you wearing wigs to alter your appearance, my poor Caroline is forever shorn of her golden hair. They're still upstairs in the attic, along with all of your trunks.

Today, I plan to visit the offices of The Denver Evening Post and do some research. Unfortunately, I cannot speak with the young woman directly because of the injuries she sustained last night. I am searching for the connection between Mrs. Miller and Mrs. VanderHelm, aside from a charity function she attended at the woman's home. Actually, I'm searching for any intersecting points. Even the mysterious benefactor, the infamous and unfortunately dead, Mr. Larson, provides no connectivity.

It is in times like these that I envy you most. How satisfying it must be to not only identify your miscreant but to trounce him as well! I feel a growing need to soundly trounce someone.

I look forward to the holidays when you have promised to visit. I have been concocting some fragrant bath salts with the petals of our heavenly Dupuy Jamain rose. They should provide a pleasant sensory experience for you.

Correspondence arrived from Mother this week with details concerning her next visit. I assume she contacted you as well because she mentioned her expectation to see you here in Denver. I think she is coming to understand the demands and the transient nature of your profession.

If you have the occasion, please trounce someone for me and then write to me all about it.

Love,

Rose

Rose folded the typed letter into the envelope and reached

down to scratch the top of Sergeant's head. "Well, it looks like it's up to us to solve this. Why don't we go for a walk around the block? From the girth of you, I'm not at all sure that the neighbor boy is exercising you at all. Besides, nothing helps to jog the pieces of a mental puzzle into place like a brisk walk."

"Mrs. Pennyworth, I'm taking Sergeant for a constitutional. If anyone should phone, please take a message." Rose waited in the entry for a response. Somewhere in the vicinity of the kitchen came a familiar grunt of acknowledgment.

"Thank you, Mrs. Pennyworth," Rose called out as she grasped Sergeant's collar in her gloved hand. To the dog she announced, "You'll not be taking off with me holding the leash."

Sergeant lagged a few feet behind Rose, looking, if possible, more mournful than usual. It wasn't to be held against him as it was a hallmark of his breed to wear such a sorrowful expression. Every aspect of his features bore a downward cast. But some days he needed more encouragement than others. "Come, Sergeant. Pick up those paws. If you're in luck, you might see a cat or two."

Stretching out before them, in one long straight line, the sidewalk reminded her of the timeline she'd been walking from the first moment Mrs. VanderHelm arrived in her parlor. As she saw it now, the timeline had attached itself to her like a cumbersome tail on a kite, weighing her down, hindering her view from a higher vantage point. She could release the tail of the kite and start where last night's break-in occurred and work her way backward. She now held two pieces of vital information that deserved priority attention.

Mr. Mayhew had muttered, "Knew it would happen. Knew they'd come." The second was the ominous warning, "If you use what you know, there will be consequences."

Mr. Mayhew, the father, had expected trouble to come.

"If you use what you know, there will be consequences."

The question hung heavy in the room. What knowledge would bring such violence upon Victoria and her father?

She recalled her father's words. *"Knowledge is power."* He'd used those three words often enough to urge them to apply themselves to their studies. But aside from the empowerment Rose and Casey had gained academically, she understood in later years another meaning. Knowledge could become not only a tool but a weapon.

Rose considered all the information lawyers hold confidentially, information that could mean incarceration or worse for their clients. Was this some damning knowledge that the woman held, or was it Mr. Mayhew? With his daughter unconscious in the hospital, the visit to *The Denver Evening Post* must be the next stop in her investigation. If she could learn what type of cases Mr. Mayhew handled before his illness, a motive might become more obvious.

Mrs. Pennyworth's cheeks were flushed when she met Rose at the front door. "Dr. Whitman called a few moments ago. He says that poor unfortunate lady who got hurt last night is awake, and you should come now."

CHAPTER 17

"She's alert, but I don't want her to grow fatigued with a barrage of questions. I'm only permitting this because she called you last night. Do you understand? Detective Donahue will be displeased with both of us if he knows you were here before he had an opportunity to interview Mrs. Miller."

The woman looked pale and vulnerable on the hospital bed. Rose nodded her understanding and whispered, "I'll be sensitive. I can be, you know?" She took a step into the room.

"Be quick." Dr. Whitman positioned himself in the doorway to keep watch while Rose crossed the room to the side of the woman's bed.

"Mrs. Miller, I'm glad to see you awake," Rose said.

The young woman attempted to focus on Rose. Her pupils were strangely dilated, making them appear devoid of all color and a sharp contrast to her pale complexion.

Rose pulled up a chair. "I came as soon as I heard you'd called me last night. I'm sorry we didn't reach you before this happened."

She drew her gaze away from Rose and focused on the ceiling. Her breathing altered to a faster pace. "I shouldn't have involved you."

"But you did. Now I'm here. What happened last night?"

Victoria Miller drew the thin sheet close to her chin, clutching it as though it could protect her.

Rose tried a fresh approach. "Can you at least tell me why you wanted to see me?"

Still, she kept her eyes diverted and from the set of her jaw, Rose doubted she'd be able to glean anything from her without more time to gain her trust. She glanced at the doctor, still with his back to her, eyes focused on the hallway. It was clear she had little time for this interview.

Rose lay her hand on the sheet covering the woman's shoulder. "Mrs. Miller—Victoria—it's obvious you're in some kind of serious trouble. I want to help you and your father, if I can. But you have to talk to me. I don't have much to go on."

She closed her eyes and whispered again, "I shouldn't have involved you." Then with more urgency, "Please go."

"You know why Mrs. VanderHelm's home was broken into, don't you?" Rose knew she had little to base her statement upon. It was, at best, a guess, but if these two cases were connected, Victoria Miller was the only thread for Rose to pull. "Do you also know who?"

The widow's breath caught at the first question. She bit down hard on her bottom lip, and the skin around her mouth drained of color.

"Rose," Dr. Whitman whispered her name with a tone of urgency.

"You can trust me, Victoria. If you change your mind, call me or talk to Dr. Whitman. Will you do that?"

Nothing.

Rose patted her arm again as she stood. "I'm going to find out who did this, with or without your help." She turned for the door.

"Is my father safe?" the woman asked.

"Dr. Whitman made sure he kept a room here. He's down the hall. The doctor also said that an officer is guarding his room—for now. I don't know how long that will last unless they have some explanation for what happened."

The doctor stepped past Rose, pushing past her on his way to the bedside. As he passed, he whispered, "You went too far."

Rose stepped out into the hallway, leaving the doctor to tend to his patient. Although Victoria Miller hadn't given her anything firm to go on, her silence had opened the possibilities for additional avenues to pursue. Her visit had also confirmed the urgency to learn more about her father, Mr. Mayhew.

ROSE PUSHED A pair of wire-rimmed glasses up on the bridge of her nose and cleared her throat. The older woman guarding the desk inside *The Denver Evening Post* offices glanced up with an expression as devoid of social pleasantries as her own. As much as Casey and more recently, Dr. Whitman, had tried to school Rose in the art of congenial interactions, she continued to disappoint and frustrate them both.

The simple disguise certainly gave Rose a studious appearance that might suppress any curiosity about her inquiries into old newspaper articles.

"We have no openings," the woman said brusquely, as though Rose had made an inquiry for work.

"That's not why I've come. I work for *The Queen Bee*, and I wish to conduct some research for an article. Mrs. Churchill is quite particular about the accuracy of her newspaper in all regards."

"Mrs. Churchill's paper?" the woman looked left and right, before leaning forward and saying, "I've been a subscriber for four years." Her eyes darted left and right again, reminding Rose of a typewriter carriage return operated by a proficient typist. "It's better than the sensational articles you'll get from here." She puffed out her cheeks and blew like a horse. "There isn't a better friend to women's fight for rights than our own Mrs. Churchill."

"I couldn't agree more. We'll win the fight if we unite!" Feeling bolstered by the woman's enthusiasm, Rose relaxed and made her request. "May I see papers for the years of 1895-1898?"

The woman reacted with a snort of disbelief. "That'll be quite a stack of papers. Sure you don't want to tackle one year at a time?"

Rose did a quick mental calculation and acquiesced.

For the next hour, Rose scanned every legal trial over the year 1895, finding numerous articles. Most appeared to be fillers for the paper dealing with petty crimes ranging from shop break-ins to assault. But Mr. Mayhew's name appeared in seven high-profile cases, involving men whose names she immediately recognized. In each, he was the prosecuting attorney for the state of Colorado, losing only one due to the death of one witness prior to giving testimony.

Before Rose could remember to put on her glasses again, the woman returned with the stack of papers from 1896. "I see you read without your spectacles, too. I have a terrible time with small print these days. I find reading without them is better. It's probably these dim lights on this side of the building. It's those tight-fisted men upstairs that give the columnists the best offices with their windows opening onto Champa Street."

Another hour and another year of newspapers later, the pieces of Mr. Mayhew's career had formed a clear image of a man dedicated to seeking justice for the innocent. Mr. Mayhew might have been Rose's father, a man with the same perseverance and keen sense of right and wrong. Such a man would inspire loyalty, the fierce loyalty Rose had sensed from his daughter during their luncheon conversation.

Most of Mayhew's trials involved prosecuting those who had defrauded investors in land schemes, clever get-rich-quick offers, bogus mining claims, and an incredulous assortment of cases. The attorney's record for getting convictions was remarkable—until the last month of 1897, when three verdicts decided in favor of the defendant.

"You look like you've been assigned the kind of muck-raking

assignment I've just been handed."

Rose looked up into the grinning face of a young man with a stack of papers nearly as high as those before her. She made a quick evaluation, assuming he was a junior reporter. He'd be one of those hard-working assistants, probably relegated to tagging along behind some senior reporter, forced to do the man's legwork, dreaming of his getting own byline one day.

He juggled the stack of papers to one arm and stuck out his hand beneath them. "Jake O'Brien."

She took his proffered hand, and he awkwardly shook it, barely managing not to lose his grip on the stack. She said, "I'm—Red. Red Winchester."

He quickly pulled his hand back to steady his load. "Now that's a fantastic name for a reporter. Are you? A reporter, I mean."

"*The Queen Bee.*" It wasn't a lie, per se. She'd stated the name of a newspaper. She didn't say she worked there. Her conscience would make her suffer for it later.

"Red Winchester." He repeated the alias with his eyes rolling to the ceiling, then returned a skeptical eye to her. "But that's not your name, is it?"

"It's a pen name," Rose said without embellishment.

"What are you looking for? I saw you come in a couple of hours ago. Must be important." He dropped the stack on the edge of the worktable beside hers. *The Queen* doesn't do much reporting on much more than ladies' issues, does it?"

"Any news which is of significance to the citizens of Denver is newsworthy for Mrs. Churchill's publication. Have you ever read one of her editions, Mr. O'Brien?"

He scrubbed his cheek, his brow furrowed in confusion. "Can't say that I have. Always thought they'd be reporting on women's sewing circles or tea parties for discussing ladies' fashions."

Rose stared at him for an intense silent moment, lost for words to express her contempt at his ignorance.

"Maybe, I should read one?"

"To improve upon your deficient education, it would be prudent."

He grabbed the stack and took a few steps back. "Well, hope you find what you're looking for. As one reporter to another, if I can offer a hand with your research, just call on me. Remember my name. Jake O'Brien. You'll be hearing more from me." With that, he made an expedient exit from the room.

Rose tapped her pencil on the table in a rapid cadence. Casey would have scolded her for slipping out of character. She'd botched it, falling back into her own personality by treating the boy's ignorance with scorn. Casey would have enlightened the poor ignorant soul, not berated him. "Pish," she muttered as she resumed her research.

Besides the notes she accumulated on Mr. Mayhew, she'd noted any article which mentioned Mr. Raymond Larson. Only three referenced the man. Two mentioned him as having sold several properties to the Denver and Rio Grande narrow gauge line. The third referenced his generous donation of land upon which to establish a children's home, a charity sponsored by a woman whose husband was on the board of directors for The Silverton Loan and Trust.

She needed a greater bank of cases to substantiate her growing suspicions. While the evidence was not conclusive, there was enough to motivate her to invest another hour immersed in Denver's history. With her recall abilities, she would waste no parcel of information.

"1897?" the woman asked, examining Rose more carefully over the top of her glasses. "This must be an important article to make you invest so much time."

"It may be life-changing," Rose answered candidly.

An hour later, with one more page of her notebook filled and pleased with the information she'd gleaned, Rose stepped out into the late afternoon sunlight. After being inside the darkened interior of the *Post*'s offices, she walked the two blocks to the streetcar rather than hailing a cab. As she turned the corner onto Champa Street, a familiar prickling between her shoulder blades caused her to slow her pace. She dropped her bag and stooped to pick it up. A quick glance offered no visual evidence of her suspicion that someone tailed her, but as she continued along the sidewalk, the prickling became a persistent and uncomfortable itch.

Outside the confectioner's shop, she stopped to feign interest in a display of chocolate soldiers. Three pedestrians passed her— one, a man a few inches taller than herself, hesitated a few seconds too long. A few doors down, he ducked inside an open shop.

THE CASE OF THE PECULIAR INHERITANCE

Although unable to make out his facial features, she noted his brown coat and tan-colored hat, the latter pulled low on his brow.

Rose hurried past the shop and met up with the streetcar as it rounded the corner. As soon as she'd stepped inside the car, she leaned over to peer through a window. The man who had followed her pulled up at the corner. Even with the hat brim turned down as it was, she could see the man's lips utter a curse.

CHAPTER 18

"Our board is filling, Sergeant. I need space for a timeline." Rose drew a long horizontal line at the bottom of the board. She started in the middle and wrote Detective Donahue's name along with two circles for eyes and a frowning mouth. His sudden warning and change of heart for assisting her had to have some bearing on this case.

From that point she worked to the left, filling in brief references to each piece of evidence until she'd arrived at the end and written, "Mrs. VanderHelm's break-in."

Rose drew in a deep breath. "This isn't helping. Maybe a little Chopin. Come, Sergeant! To the parlor!"

Polished to Mrs. Pennyworth's highest standards, the mahogany piano held a prominent position in the parlor's corner. As she'd admired its beauty in a catalog three years earlier, she'd imagined the pleasant evenings she and friends would enjoy listening to its elegant tones and pleasuring in the rhapsodies of the masters. She had not yet garnered the audience she'd imagined. But like her persistence in all academic matters, she applied herself with alacrity, although not as often as the instrument might require for mastery.

She slipped onto the piano bench and scanned the page from Chopin's Prelude in E-Minor, Opus 28. Rose flexed her fingers above the keys, closed her eyes, and imagined the lilting tune as she'd heard it played years ago in Chicago. Although a simple melody, for a novice like Rose, it presented a satisfying challenge, one she'd yet to master.

Sergeant, curled in the center of the Oriental rug on the opposite side of the room, lay with his ears flopped out on either side of his head, his eyes closed. Rose had noticed his reluctance to sit closer whenever she played, thinking it a curious behavior.

She pressed her fingers to the keys, swaying with the sweet familiar melody. The muscles in her neck relaxed, and she hummed along. "Da, da, da, da, da, da, dum, da, da, da, da, da. Dum, da, da, da, da . . ." Rose lifted her hands, holding them suspended above the keys. Her eyes sprang open as she listened to a low vibration. It ceased so abruptly, she reasoned she'd imagined it.

She played the first stanza again, this time joining in with her own voice, echoing the notes. "Da, da, da, da, da, da, dum, da, da, da, da, da. Dum, da, da, da, da, dum . . ." She lifted her hands from the keys and looked about the room. But just as before, the unusual sound stopped at the same time.

Rose resumed the prelude. As before, the strange ghostly moaning began as well. Sergeant opened his eyes, pulled himself to his feet, stretched, and swung his head in her direction before padding from the room. It might have been pure imagination, but

Sergeant's eyes suggested disapproval or boredom. Rose never could decide which.

Before Rose began a fourth time, Mrs. Pennyworth stepped into the room. "I'm heading to bed now. Anything else you need before I retire for the night?"

"No thank you, Mrs. Pennyworth. I can take care of anything I might need."

"Well then, good night. I trust you won't be up much longer playing that tune."

"I'll just finish this piece before retiring."

"Thank the heavens," Mrs. Pennyworth said, turning to go.

"Oh, one thing. Was there any more of your apple cake remaining?"

Mrs. Pennyworth answered, "I put it in the icebox out of Sergeant's reach."

"Very good. Thank you. Have a pleasant rest."

Mrs. Pennyworth's heels clicked along the hallway, growing fainter until Rose heard her bedroom door open at the back of the house. Not for the first time, Rose considered her good fortune at finding such a fine housekeeper and excellent cook all in one person.

Rose returned to Chopin's Prelude and lifted her hands above the keys. She took another slow inhale and closed her eyes as she lowered her left hand. With the softest of pressure, she stroked the key.

Briinng.

Her eyes flew open, staring in confusion at the keyboard. She blinked and pressed the key again, rewarded by a perfect *b*. Another sound drifted from the entry hall, followed by a light *swish*.

"Mrs. Pennyworth?"

Rose walked to the front door where a large envelope lay wedged beneath it. She opened the door and peered out onto the darkened street.

"How deliciously mysterious!" She retrieved an envelope from the floor and closed the door behind her. No address. No return.

She tucked the envelope beneath her arm and headed for the kitchen. A piece of apple cake and a secret, late-night delivery made a delightful combination! She poured herself a cup of milk and set it on the table along with a fork and knife. Upon opening the icebox, the fragrance of cinnamon and apples met her, inviting indulgence. Perched on a stool at the end of the kitchen counter, she picked up the knife, then considered the trouble of washing it. She chose the fork instead and took a bite.

Four bites later, she turned her attention to the sealed envelope. The knife served its purpose by becoming a letter opener. Inside were two sheets of ordinary typing paper, with no note of explanation. She took a delicate sip of milk.

The paper, typewritten and double-spaced on both sides, held no clues to suggest its origin. Within moments of reading, she understood that each line of type detailed a criminal charge made against Raymond Larson. Along with the dates of each charge, a simple explanation followed along with the person or persons making the complaint.

Rose lay her fork down and picked up the paper in two hands, studying each name and mentally correlating it with the newspaper articles she had found today. Out of the two pages of charges lodged with the police, she'd seen only three make it to trial.

She read the handwritten note at the bottom of the second page. "These cases were never prosecuted due to disturbingly similar reasons: either the witness disappeared, lost their memory of the incident, or died."

Rose picked up her fork and took another bite, chewing slowly while she processed this latest information. She sipped at her milk as the pieces slipped neatly into place. "Detective Donahue, I believe I have you to thank for this."

Evidently, the detective thought he was protecting her by shutting her out of the official investigation. He well knew what happened to people who involved themselves with Mr. Larson, an unhealthy and often-deadly association.

To have evaded justice for so long meant that the man wielded a great deal of influence with those even more powerful. The man had become untouchable by intimidating an entire legal system.

Her father's voice whispered from her memories. *Knowledge is power.* "How did you evade the long arm of justice all of your life? What knowledge did you possess, Mr. Larson

CHAPTER 19

"I'm sorry. I know you want to speak with both of them, but I don't think it's wise to question her father now. He's in a fragile state of mind, not to mention how much this entire situation has further strained his heart."

"Surely the police have interrogated him?" Rose said, frustrated to the point of risking her friend's ire.

"Yes, but you aren't with the police, are you?"

Dr. Whitman cupped Rose's elbow and led her away. At the end of the hall, he stopped before a window overlooking the hospital's rose garden. "Mrs. Miller has made clear her wishes not to speak to anyone, including you. In fact, her instructions specifically mentioned you."

Rose crossed her arms and gazed out on the circular stone path winding through a sea of roses. This was not the time to give into anger born of frustration. She asked in as calm a voice as she could muster, "Will they dismiss this case because they found nothing stolen, just like they did at Mrs. VanderHelm's home?"

"I've seen Detective Donahue several times over the past two days, so I think I can safely say his investigation is ongoing." The doctor took a step closer and pushed a strand of her hair behind her ear, studying her with obvious concern. "Have you been able to sleep?"

"If you're about to tell me I look a fright, I may plant the toe of my boot in your shin."

The doctor smiled charmingly and whispered, "I would never say you look anything but lovely." His smile turned impish. "Even with those dark circles under your attractive blue eyes."

She ignored his comment, choosing to change the topic. "I came upon some interesting newspaper articles yesterday that have led my investigation to travel in an entirely different direction." She reached into her handbag and tugged the folded papers from under her revolver.

The doctor's face dissolved into a scowl when he caught sight of the gun. "Why are you carrying that now? We're in a hospital, for goodness sakes."

"Why did Detective Donahue put a guard at the doors to both Mr. Mayhew and Mrs. Miller's rooms if there wasn't a potential threat?"

"I see your point." He gestured to the papers. "What's this, then?"

"A gift." She lowered her voice. "From a friend. The same friend I thought had abandoned me two nights ago. Someone slipped it under my door last night."

Dr. Whitman's eyes widened. "Donahue?"

"I can't say for certain they were from him, but who else would drop on my doorstep a file listing charges against Mr. Larson, a man of particular interest in this case?"

"Hmm. So, the implication is that you were correct to assume a connection between all three break-ins." He tapped the papers in her hands. "According to this, they have an additional tie to the infamous Mr. Larson?"

"Exactly."

"But Mrs. VanderHelm?"

"Obviously, her role in this is minor, maybe even accidental," Rose said, more convinced now that she said it aloud. As she had finished Mrs. Pennyworth's apple cake last night, it was the only logical conclusion.

Dr. Whitman pulled out his pocket watch and after glancing down the hall said, "There's another doctor on the floor. I've got the time. Why don't we go for a stroll?"

Denver's autumn had turned pleasantly warm again, and under a bright sun the roses fairly glowed. Rose bent to sniff the clear pink blossom of a Minden rose. She closed her eyes, locking into her memory its delicate fragrance. "I think we both agree that she isn't the type to associate with Mr. Larson. She told us that first day she had no acquaintance with the man. From the beginning, she stated she believed the gift to be a mistake. I should have realized it then."

"All right." He wrapped his arm through hers and they fell into step. "If they, whoever they might be, intended the vase for someone else, then who was that someone?"

Rose shook her head and said, "It's more than a question of who."

He stopped and turned with a questioning look.

She reached down to stroke the gray-green foliage of a tea rose. "I haven't pieced it all together. But I don't think the motive for the break-in was the vase but maybe something in the vase. Something significant to those who knew Raymond Larson."

"All right. So, I suppose we would ask what might be important to Raymond Larson."

Rose tucked a white petal into her pocket, then tapped her bag. "Because of what I learned from my mysterious friend who gave me these papers, I can assume it was information—useful information to those inclined to larceny."

He stared at her a moment, and she watched as awareness brightened his eyes. "Blackmail!"

Rose shushed him and gave him a nod as she took his arm again. "You may make a detective yet, Dr. Whitman."

"So, the information they were seeking wasn't in the vase, and they made a second break-in the following night?" he asked.

"That's what it looks like on the surface. But there are so many dissimilar aspects to the break-ins. The mode of entry for one. I'm convinced an experienced burglar committed the first, yet the more recent intruder forced an entry through the window, as would an amateur."

"The first entry made a mess of the downstairs rooms, while the second almost tidy," he said.

"Yes, they took nothing. So, I must assume they were looking for the same thing."

"The vase," he said.

THE CASE OF THE PECULIAR INHERITANCE

"No."

"Something in the vase, then? Something hidden?" Dr. Whitman asked.

"If it was there, then why a third break-in of Mrs. Miller's house?"

"You have no solid evidence to say these are connected. I suppose it could be a coincidence that you became involved in three break-ins in the same week." He turned to her with a lopsided smile. "That would be quite a coincidence, wouldn't it?"

"I think so, and so did Detective Donahue. Remember what he said that night about not having any break-ins in a month? No, they're connected. Then there is the note. The note takes us back to the explanation that this string of break-ins is about finding some piece or pieces of information. Something Raymond Larson possessed until his death."

"Then it was stolen and for some bizarre reason, hidden inside—a package which someone mistakenly delivered to the wrong person." The doctor narrowed his eyes. "That sounds to me like a poorly plotted work of fiction."

Rose ignored his remark and continued her speculation. "Maybe the person who hid it couldn't chance taking it from the man's house. After all, there were probably several people from the auction house involved in crating those items."

"With a stretch of imagination, I suppose that could explain why it ended up in a vase or whatever it was in."

"Right now, I'm more interested in Mrs. Miller's role in all of this," Rose said. "One I believe is significant."

Dr. Whitman glanced over his shoulder, and as he did, his hand brushed against a thorny stem. "Ouch!" He pulled a handkerchief from his pocket and dabbed at the back of his hand. "How can something so beautiful inflict such pain?"

Rose opened her mouth to propose a philosophical reply but thought better of it. After his suggestion that her theories were more suited for fictional narratives than sound investigative analysis, she thought it best to let the opportunity pass. Too bad, though, because she had a splendidly witty comeback.

Dr. Whitman blotted the blood from his hand while Rose continued her conjecture. "Mrs. Miller was involved in the man's estate settlements and probably had access to the house. The man who attacked her knew that and assumed she had the—let's call them documents."

He took her arm again and gamely jumped into the narrative with his own analysis. "So, she might have them. Whoever wrote the note presumed she had some vital information." He glanced up at the second-floor hospital window where they'd stood moments ago. "That's why Detective Donahue posted a guard. He's thinking there will be another assault."

"Perhaps. He is using them both as bait." Rose dismissed the idea that Detective Donahue would have devised such a plan, but there was the real possibility that a superior officer might have. When the doctor didn't respond to her notion of using his patients as bait, Rose looked over at him. He fixed his eyes on a bend in the pathway behind them. "What is it?" she asked.

"There's a man I swear has been following us. Maybe it's just .

THE CASE OF THE PECULIAR INHERITANCE

..but considering what's been happening, he makes me uneasy."

"Can you describe him?"

"He's always been just out of range for me to get a good look, but his height and build remind me of someone I saw this morning chatting with one of the floor nurses."

Before he could stop her, Rose retraced their path through the garden. Behind her, the doctor ran to catch up.

At their point of entrance into the garden, the doctor caught up to her. "He's gone by now. He must have known I saw him," he said.

"How likely is it that the man we saw at Mrs. Miller's house, the man stumbling down that staircase, bleeding from a gunshot wound, would be up and walking so soon?"

He rubbed the back of his neck and frowned. "From the amount of blood we found at the break-in, I doubt that he'd have the strength."

Rose pressed her teeth against her lower lip as she considered the remaining possibilities. "So, there's more than one person with an interest in recovering the information. If Raymond Larson was blackmailing enough people to keep himself out of prison all these years, half of Denver's lawyers, judges, and police force could be searching for those documents."

The doctor continued Rose's speculations. "Because if they fell into the hands of an unscrupulous person—"

"The blackmailing would continue. Because knowledge is power." Rose wrapped her arm through the doctor's, and they started back for the hospital's entrance. "Victoria Miller is the key to all of this. She has to be."

"She's certainly involved in something unhealthy."

Rose turned to determine if the doctor was teasing, but she saw no hint of intended humor in his eyes. "Only you, Dr. Whitman, would refer to her precarious position in such a fashion."

After they'd checked in on both Mr. Mayhew and Mrs. Miller, the doctor escorted Rose to the stairwell. "I'm sorry my words offended you yesterday. I will not apologize for saying them. I would rather you not take risks. Unfortunately, I know you won't stop until you've worked out this mystery. Could this be why you love that old hound dog of yours? You share a similar trait. You've picked up the scent, and nothing will stop you until you get to the end of the trail."

"Such a romantic analogy, doctor. I shall cherish your comparison of myself to my dog."

CHAPTER 20

Moments later as Rose stepped out of the hospital, she nearly collided with a man who approached the steps carrying a lavish bouquet of yellow and peach dahlias. "Mr. Kent! I didn't see you behind those exquisite flowers."

The lawyer stepped to the side, a moment of confusion in his expression, followed by slow recognition. "Miss McKenzie. Hello."

"I assume you're here to visit, Mrs. Miller," Rose said.

"Uh, yes. I just learned about what happened. Shocking news. I probably wouldn't have known, it being a weekend. But the police came to my home, asking questions. I didn't know until a few hours ago." He lowered the bouquet. A look of puzzlement and genuine concern crossed his face. "And you? Did you come to visit Mrs. Miller, too?"

Rose nodded. "I've just come from her room, in fact. Unfortunately, she's only recently come to."

"Come to? She was unconscious?" The bouquet dropped to his side. "I hadn't heard that her injuries were so severe."

"Dr. Whitman is an excellent physician. He's attending her, so she's in expert hands." She studied the man's stunned reaction and hypothesized plausible explanations as they aligned with his relationship to the young woman. He might be simply an empathetic employer or his response could be indicative of a romantic relationship. "I'm sure the beautiful bouquet will please her when she awakens."

His gaze dropped to the flowers, then back to Rose. "This is terrible news."

His face appeared more pallid than when they'd first met, as if he'd been ill. But that meeting was only a few days ago. "Indeed. Mrs. Miller told me you knew her father, as well."

"Um, yes. We'd had occasion to work together . . . those years when he was practicing, of course," Kent said, "It's good of you to come to visit Mrs. Miller considering you scarcely know her."

Rose considered her response with utmost prudence. A statement could often be interpreted as a question, especially when followed by such an expectant pause. "She actually called me the night of the attack. Dr. Whitman and I went to her home at her request." Rose used her own dramatic sense of timing before she finished. "She said that it was urgent she speak with me."

"How . . . unusual. Something urgent?"

The man's face became a mask. Her father could perform the same feat of magic and appear enigmatic when occasion required it. She'd always assumed it was a learned defense mechanism. Perhaps, with just enough information, she would catch the attorney's genuine reaction.

"The assailant was in the home when we arrived," she said.

"He was? How frightening for you! What did you do? Did you see him?"

"He ran past us as he fled from the house."

Kent slipped naturally into his own investigative mode, thinking as an attorney would in such situations. "That means you could identify the man." It wasn't a question.

"Unfortunately, the interior of the house was too dark to make out more than the vague impression that he was shorter than myself. He was bent over, stumbling down the stairs, you see."

He frowned, and she read his unspoken question.

"Mrs. Miller appeared to have shot him."

"Shot him?"

"We think she expected him and had armed herself." Rose stated the revelation with sufficient dramatic timing that she felt confident Casey would have approved.

"Excuse me." A young man came between Rose and the attorney on their way to the front door. "Thank you."

The untimely happenstance blocked her view of Kent's reaction.

"I'm shocked that this should have happened to someone like Mrs. Miller and her father. Is Mr. Mayhew unharmed?"

"Fortunately, it appears he will make a full recovery."

"That's good. That's excellent. Well, you've certainly had a time of it, too. Unharmed, aside from the obvious shock of such an encounter?"

"I'm fine, thank you." Her opportunity had passed. Apart

from the continued pallor of his complexion, the attorney had composed himself.

"Well, then. I suppose I've detained you long enough." He touched a finger to the brim of his hat, then asked, "Oh, how is your investigation going concerning the gift received by Mrs. VanderHelm?"

"I'm ruling out the earliest suspects, and I believe I'll be closing in on the actual perpetrator soon." Rose headed down the sidewalk, feeling quite pleased with herself for managing the last word and making an adroit departure.

The four blocks required to catch the streetcar home gave her time to reflect on her conversation with Kent and her speculations about Mrs. Miller. The rhythmic tap of her heels on the sidewalk helped slow the spinning cogs of her brain. She liked to think of her brain resembling an elaborate clockwork, resplendent when all was ticking efficiently with shiny brass gears, meshing against cogs. Tick-tock, tick-tock, her heels clicking against the solid pavement, matching the systematic review of clues and possibilities.

Much of what she'd told the doctor she held as indisputable; a smaller portion had been conjecture. Her suspicions that Mrs. Miller had been responsible for the second break-in to Mrs. VanderHelm's house she'd kept to herself. Rose believed it, not only unlikely but preposterous, that the serious young widow would have climbed through a window and searched the home like a common thief.

With the wires of the streetcar coming into view at the next intersection, Rose experienced an unpleasant prickling between her shoulder blades. She glanced over her shoulder, but a dozen pedestrians behind her on the crowded walkway provided no obvious danger. She picked up her pace.

Street traffic flowed in an erratic pattern, meaning there was little chance to gauge one's chances of crossing the street with any assurance of not being run down by a horse and rider, horse and cart, or horse and carriage. Lanes were arbitrary and speed of travel was whatever your animal's age or enthusiasm could attain. Crossing any Denver street in the middle of the day required iron nerves or a certain measure of recklessness. Neither of these attributes were lacking in Rose so she lifted her skirt, stepped off the sidewalk, and wove her way to the opposite side of the street without mishap.

Once safely on the sidewalk, she stepped to a large storefront window providing a perfect reflection of the street she'd just crossed. A tall man wearing a duster and wide-brimmed hat charged into the street and began the treacherous passage, nearly trampled by a nervous mule pulling a meat wagon. He leaped up onto the sidewalk and in that unguarded moment, she saw him clearly—a fox-like countenance, ruddy complexion, black hair, untrimmed beard, and a long thin nose. His dark eyes locked on hers, and he smiled at her reflection. She recognized him. When she turned, he'd disappeared into the crowd.

CHAPTER 21

When Rose arrived home, she found Sergeant collapsed like melted butter on the porch step. "Why did Mrs. Pennyworth leave you here?"

The hound's dark eyes rolled up to stare at her in a more mournful manner than usual. The rest of him remained immobile, a puddle of misery.

Rose knelt beside him, giving his head a vigorous rubbing. "What did you do, Sergeant?" That's when the odor hit her full force, along with a visual evidence of thick, foul-looking mud on all four paws. She leaped to her feet and took two steps back. The hound flattened even more into his puddle of shame.

"Sergeant, come." Rose didn't wait to see if he'd follow, nor did she announce his impending bath. Neither did she wait until she'd changed her clothes, a fact that Mrs. Pennyworth pointed out at great volume from the kitchen window.

Mrs. Pennyworth dropped a pile of rags on the back porch next to Rose, where she scrubbed vigorously at Sergeant's mud-covered paw. "The neighbor boy told me the hound got away from him when that cat crossed their path. Said he ran straight through the marshy area behind the Thacker's place."

Rose pushed herself to her feet and brushed ineffectively at the mud streaking her skirt. "Well, no long-term harm done." She looked up sharply. "Unless, the cat..."

"No, the cat managed an escape."

Sergeant took that moment to shake himself. Mrs. Pennyworth yowled indignantly and stepped back.

It was a good time to retreat. Rose called for Sergeant to follow, then announced in a tone as casual as she could muster, "I'll be in the bath for approximately one hour. Please take a message if anyone calls."

The housekeeper gaped at her. "In the middle of the day? Without lunch?"

Rose expected the admonishment to come. "Yes, to both questions. Would you mind putting two of those delicious beef sandwiches you served us last night on a plate and bringing them upstairs, please?"

Mrs. Pennyworth appeared absolutely scandalized, as though Rose had announced she'd be reenacting Lady Godiva's ride through Denver. "Bring them into the bath?"

"Yes, if you please," Rose said as she stepped through the back door with Sergeant padding at her heels.

"Surely, you're not taking the dog in there with you?" the housekeeper called after her.

"Why not? He's perfectly clean."

Rose tested the temperature with her toe, before sprinkling rose petals from the garden into the steaming bathwater. From a delicate, etched glass jar, she scooped a rounded spoonful of salts laden with the fragrance of lavender. Then dropping her satin robe, she slipped into the clawfoot tub.

With a deep sigh, she immersed herself in decadent luxury. Rose closed her eyes, breathed deeply, and sank to the level of her chin. After years of practice, she stilled her mind and slipped into a meditative state.

Moments later, the knock at the door shattered her blissful state.

"Miss Rose, I have your sandwiches. Shall I put the tray on the bed?"

"No. Please bring them in here."

The door eased open, and half of Mrs. Pennyworth's head appeared. "Surely, you don't want me to leave them where that dog can get to them." She glowered at Sergeant, blissfully curled up on the rug.

Rose sat up and wiggled her fingers at the dog. "Come here, Sergeant." The dog lifted his chin as Rose scratched the silky fur along his sagging jowls. "Just put the tray on the stool, there within reach. Thank you."

Mrs. Pennyworth set the tray down and stuck her fists against her hips. "That dog's unsanitary."

"He's fine. You saw for yourself that he had a bath." Rose picked up a quarter of a sandwich and tore off a piece of beef. Sergeant's nose twitched, his eyes locked on the sandwich. "Just a bite. I won't have you turning into a sausage like the doctor's dog."

The housekeeper unceremoniously plucked Rose's soiled skirt and blouse from the back of the chair. "Are you wearing these again?"

"Of course."

Mrs. Pennyworth extended them at arm's length. "If this stink doesn't wash out, you'll know why I asked." With that, she left them, closing the door with sufficient force to jar the bar of chamomile soap from the rim of the tub into the water with a splash.

Rose fed Sergeant another corner of her sandwich. "She's quite talented at dramatic sorties, isn't she?" Retrieving the soap from the bottom of the tub proved a slippery problem, but after a third try, she set the bar on the stool beside the sandwich tray. It promptly slid to the floor where Sergeant clamped his mouth on it and just as quickly spat it out.

As she watched the soap slide beneath the tub, a vision of Mr. Charles Kent came to mind. The attorney she'd met again today at the hospital was altered in temperament from the man who'd had so little information to offer her about Mr. Larson.

Confidentiality was a definite consideration for any attorney, but Kent's vague answers would have led anyone to think he'd scarcely spoken with his client. Larson *was* his client. Even within the public record, there was more to the man than what Charles Kent shared. The lawyer might have at least repeated what the papers reported of him.

On the surface, Mr. Larson appeared an upstanding citizen, even a charitably minded one. One could make the case that the other reports of suggested impropriety had resulted from misunderstandings or malicious slander. But if Kent took the witness stand, and they forced him to answer questions such as Rose had asked, surely a judge would accuse him of prevarication.

Mrs. Pennyworth opened the door a crack and said, "Miss Rose, a letter just arrived. Do you want me to put it on your desk?"

"Is it from Casey?"

"Looks like it."

"Would you bring it here, please?"

The housekeeper stared at her, aghast. "You're reading it in the tub? While you're sitting there without your clothes on?"

Perplexed, Rose said, "Well, yes."

"But that's like . . . I mean, you're holding it up and you're *naked*."

"Oh, for goodness sakes, hand me the letter." Rose reached for her towel, wrapped it around her body, and stepped out of the tub.

> *Dear Red,*
>
> *Your latest case sounds intriguing. A crime without a motive is pretty unusual, but I have faith in your powers of deduction to have found one by the time you receive this letter.*
>
> *The doll trunk brings back some wonderful memories.*

THE CASE OF THE PECULIAR INHERITANCE

I don't know if I ever told you how I used to hide things in mine. If you found my hiding place, you never told me. Do you remember those green hair ribbons you treasured and lost? That was me, baby sister. I confess I stole them from the dresser on your birthday. I was jealous of the attention you got from our cousin Jonathan, and so I stole them. If you go up to the attic and look inside, you'll find the place in the lining where I cut a long slit. I used the knife Father gave me for Christmas that year. Unless I'm mistaken, the ribbons should still be there. I know you haven't forgiven me for Caroline's hair bob, but you must forgive me for stealing your ribbons because now you can wear them again.

I'm looking forward to Christmas with you this year, more than I can say. I've been traveling so much that all I can think about is a nice long soak in that amazing bathtub. I may not get out until 1900.

Love,
Casey

After reading the letter a second time, Rose tossed her towel over the rim of the tub and quickly drew on her silk dressing gown. She called to the dog, ignoring the guilty look in his eyes, and the empty plate beside him. "Come Sergeant! We have a case to solve." The hound's tongue took one last swipe at the crumbs and trotted through the door behind her.

Rose pulled the small trunk in which the vase had been

delivered from behind the upholstered chair in the study where Mrs. Pennyworth had given it a temporary home.

She lifted the lid and examined the fabric interior for anything similar to what Casey described. She ran her fingers along the lid where the oak exterior met with the cotton lining. Nothing obvious revealed itself. She frowned and examined the sides in the same manner, running her fingertips along the small brads and adhesive that held the lining snugly in place.

From visual examination, the bottom lining of the trunk looked as secure as the sides and lid. She ran her fingers across the fabric and stopped as the cloth gave way, offering less resistance. Pressing the area produced the distinct sound of crinkling of paper. Rose closed the lid and carried the trunk to the table. With utmost care, she slid her fingernail along the seams, only finding what she searched for on the fourth side—a clean cut along the length of the trunk's bottom lining nearly imperceptible to the eye. This time, feeling the papers hidden beneath, she made a quiet cry of triumph.

Rose extracted three sheets of paper, filled with a man's handwriting. The variety of inks and pen-tip sizes he'd used suggested he had added the lines of script at various times, perhaps spanning years—years of accumulated knowledge. She crossed the room to the stronger light near the window and scanned the papers, shaking her head with each addition of scandal and impropriety recorded by a man who knew how to use such small and big indiscretions for his own advantage. She gave a grunt of disgust and folded the papers once again, setting them on the worktable as though they might carry some infectious disease.

She stared at the discolored paper, imagining all the pain that this collected knowledge had inflicted over the years—the crimes that had gone unpunished because of threats of reprisal to those who might testify in court—the paper soiled as the hands that had used them to blackmail and extort. These three sheets of paper were all the motive anyone would need for anything, including murder.

"Miss McKenzie."

Rose jumped at the sound of her housekeeper's voice.

"There's a lady downstairs to see you. She looks a bit pale, so I sat her down in the parlor with a cup of tea before I came up to tell you. I think it's that lady that called you, the lawyer's assistant. Kind of strange acting, and she's pale as moonlight."

"Mrs. Miller is here?" Rose looked back at the papers she held, the motive for which she'd been searching, and smiled. "Tell her, I'll be right down." She reinserted the papers beneath the lining but stopped herself, pulling them free again. If she figured out where they were, someone else might have. Whoever hid them inside knew exactly where to find them. They just needed to retrieve the trunk.

Well, Mrs. Miller was just the one to answer her questions, and the junior assistant had conveniently come to her. She closed the lid of the trunk, refolded the papers, and carefully placed them into her robe pocket. For whatever reason, she felt better having them on her person. Dr. Whitman would probably accuse her of risk-taking, but so be it.

From the downstairs hallway, the phone jangled enthusiastically. Rose heard Mrs. Pennyworth answer the call. "I'll go get her right away."

Rose met her on the stairs. "Who is it?"

Mrs. Pennyworth leaned forward, whispering, "It's Dr. Whitman. He's most insistent on talking with you." Then she gave Rose's robe a disparaging glance. "You're taking visitors in that?"

Rose whispered back, "I'm going to talk to Dr. Whitman in it, too." She leaned closer to her housekeeper's ear and murmured, "And I'm wearing absolutely nothing underneath."

With a tired voice conveying his dismay, the doctor explained that his patient had convinced one of his colleagues to release her from the hospital. "I don't know where she went."

Rose spoke quietly into the receiver. "I do. She's currently in my parlor."

"What?"

Rose moved the earpiece a few inches farther from her ear. "She came to see me. I assume she's willing to explain a few things I haven't unraveled. I have to go." Leaving him no opportunity to ask further questions, she said a cheerful goodbye and hung up the phone.

She stood there a moment longer, then picked up the phone again. "Western Union? Yes, I need to send a telegram—to Miss Cassandra McKenzie."

CHAPTER 22

"Mrs. Miller, I'm so surprised to see you up and about." Rose glided into the room with her hand extended. She rather liked the ease at which she could move about, unencumbered by excess clothing. She waved her hand as the younger woman attempted to stand. "No, please, don't rise. You've been through quite an ordeal."

Mrs. Miller collapsed back into the soft cushions of Rose's sofa. "Thank you for seeing me. I'd like to apologize for being so curt with you before."

"I completely understand your reluctance to be candid with me. This is a serious matter, and what do you really know about me? I'd be distrustful, too, knowing what you do."

Mrs. Miller gazed at her wonderingly.

"Would it put your mind at ease if I were to tell you what I believe to be the events that precipitated the attack in your home?" Rose asked gently. In deference to the woman's nervous state, she thought it best to proceed as though she'd already confessed her role. Where Rose's deductions failed, she believed the woman would correct.

Mrs. Miller dropped her gaze to her hands. A single tear made a track along her cheek, pausing at the corner of her lips before sliding to her jaw and falling onto the back of her hand.

"I haven't worked out all the details because there is little evidence to prove my theories. Let's work backward from what happened in your home. The intruder suspected you had some valuable information he wanted. That's why he sent the note warning you he was coming for it. He wanted to intimidate you." Rose didn't see the need to ask her to confirm or deny this part of her narrative, based on the irrefutable proof of the evidence she possessed.

"The intruder knew you had taken this information from the estate of Mr. Larson. I haven't quite worked out how, but someone saw you take it." Rose remained attentive to the woman's physical reaction, but she sat with a rigid posture any artist would have envied in a model. "I also hypothesized that he was the intruder who entered Mrs. VanderHelm's house the first night. But it wasn't the blue vase he was after. It was what he believed to be inside it."

When Rose had yet to see any reaction, she continued her narrative. "Let's go back along the timeline to the night you broke into Mrs. VanderHelm's house."

A slight muscular twitch along the woman's jawline was the only sign that Mrs. Miller had not turned to stone.

"The fingerprints and small footprints I found gave me reason to suspect this intruder was a woman or a youth. She left fingerprints on the windowsill in blood. The cut I saw on your hand the night of your attack was fresh, but not recent enough to have occurred the night you fended off the intruder from your home. The intruder had also made the footprints with a woman's shoe, a stylish one. In fact, similar to the ones you're wearing now. I believe you entered Mrs. VanderHelm's home in search of the documents you'd taken from Mr. Larson. But you didn't find them."

Mrs. Miller's shoulders sagged. "I wanted to prove he murdered my husband. Wouldn't you have done the same if this happened to someone you loved? Wouldn't you do anything to find those responsible?"

Rose sat back, stunned. She'd assumed her motive was to restore her father's reputation. She had proof written on the papers folded inside her pocket that he was being blackmailed. She hadn't considered the young widow's husband being involved. "But Larson was blackmailing your father."

"He was!" she said crossly. "Along with half the lawyers and judges of Denver." She sat forward, her face contorted with rage. "Larson was a loathsome man, and I had to pretend to be cajoled by his flattery while I attended to the last changes to his will. But it was an opportunity I couldn't let pass. I'd learned of the file from my husband's best friend, Phillip. While he was clerking for Professor Ackerman, he'd overheard a conversation about a file that Raymond Larson kept hidden in his home."

Agitated and no longer able to maintain her initial composure,

Mrs. Miller rose to her feet and paced to the piano and back again, her arms gesticulating with nervous energy. "Phillip was always a skilled conversationalist. We imagined he'd win any case he argued simply on his oratory skills." She stopped and glanced at Rose as though she'd forgotten where her story was leading. "He should never have told his roommate." Her voice grew small. "A reporter for *The Denver Times* wrote an article about a mysterious file kept on dozens of prominent leaders of Denver society. It was vague and never cited a source. It never mentioned the name of Raymond Larson. That last bit of information Phillip had only shared with my husband, Patrick, and myself.

"When they found the reporter in an alley dead from a gunshot wound to the head, Phillip panicked. He told Patrick he had to leave town. That they'd find him." She stopped pacing and stood like a statue once more, grief etched on her youthful face. "Patrick accompanied Phillip that night to the train station. My husband just wanted to make sure his friend made it out of town safely." Her voice broke.

As difficult as it was, Rose remained silent, waiting out the long periods as the distraught woman recalled the events. But she now appeared frozen beyond all ability to continue. Rose felt a stab of sympathy and crossed the room, wrapping her arm around the widow's shoulders. "I think you should sit down."

Mrs. Miller lifted her glistening eyes to Rose, and in them, Rose saw the story's ending. "You don't have to say more. It's enough for me to understand that your motive was to seek justice for someone you loved." Rose felt her throat tighten as memories of her own father's untimely death swept over her. "I understand that need."

In a small, strained voice, the widow said, "Phillip and Patrick appeared so alike. Same height, build, and coloring. They used a streetcar to kill my Patrick. They say he fell on the tracks. Phillip disappeared." She covered her face with her hands and finished between shuddering sobs. "Patrick didn't have an accident. I'm certain they murdered him."

CHAPTER 23

"There you go, dear." Mrs. Pennyworth refilled Victoria Miller's cup with what she called her *special tea*. Rose knew it to be a powerful restorative elixir of lemon juice and something quite stronger. Whatever else she added to it, she made it a palatable potion. "I toasted a few biscuits for you, and that's my raspberry jam on top." She patted the widow's shoulder. "Try to take some nourishment."

"Thank you, Mrs. Pennyworth. That was very thoughtful of you." Rose warmed to her housekeeper's display of compassion. But when the housekeeper cast yet another censorious glance at Rose's robe, the moment passed.

Mrs. Miller idly fingered her cup before saying, "Because there was no evidence, the police said that his death was nothing more than an accident."

"You never saw the papers?"

"Not until I was in Raymond Larson's home a week before he died." She took a tentative sip from her cup, followed quickly by a second longer one. "He knew he was dying, but he still behaved as though he had some magnetic charisma, joking at his success in every enterprise he set his mind to, including women."

"I still don't understand why Mr. Kent would send an assistant to take care of something as critical as changes to his estate. Why didn't he go himself?" Rose asked, as her suspicions pivoted to consider a new line of possibilities.

"Mr. Kent told me that Larson distrusted nearly everyone, exhibiting extreme paranoia."

Rose nodded. "Considering the number of people he'd ruined over the years, he had a reason to fear reprisals. But why you? I'm not trying to suggest you lack ability, but you are, by your own admittance, inexperienced."

"I asked the same thing, but it was more than I'd hoped for—an opportunity to, at the very least, see the papers and the evidence that could ruin my father. But I also hoped to find proof of his involvement in the death of my husband."

"I'm sorry to persist on this point, but what other reason did Mr. Kent give for sending you?"

Mrs. Miller gave a sardonic smile. "Because he knew Larson would be more comfortable working with a pretty young woman, I suspect. Mr. Kent told me of angry encounters between the two of them and the paranoia that had gripped Larson in the last months. So, I played my role and got what I wanted. Three days before his death, he was disagreeable. His mood made it difficult for me to get him to focus on signing critical papers. I think he realized any control over his life was over, and he wanted to impress me."

She took another long drink, wincing as she did. "He told me to look in his desk, and then he described how to open the false bottom in the center drawer. I pulled out the file folder and started to take it back to him, but he stopped me halfway across the room. That's when he asked me to open it and read off the names of all the men and women he owned. Owned! That's what he said. I think I could have killed him in that moment. It crossed my mind. God help me, but it did." Turning a defiant look at Rose, she asked, "Have you ever hated anyone that much?"

Rose recognized the question for what it was—a rhetorical statement. But unlike Victoria Miller, who felt shame for such thinking, Rose did not. She knew the festering wound caused by her father's murder would never heal until justice found those still living with his blood on their hands.

"I'd found what I'd come for, the dirty file. For those few minutes I held in my hands the answers I was seeking, the chance to restore my father's ability to practice law again and vindication for my husband's murder."

"But you couldn't take them until the man was dead," Rose finished.

"I knew I'd need to work quickly once he died because there'd be those who'd want the file to continue Larson's blackmailing."

Rose poured herself a cup of tea, holding the cup below her nose, fortified by the fragrance of bergamot. "May I test my theory about what happened next?"

Mrs. Miller gave a small shrug of her shoulder. "If you wish.

I'm too tired to explain more."

"When you arrived at the house, the men from the auction company were already on the grounds. You explained your presence as necessary to ensure that certain items intended as gifts to family and friends were marked and set aside. When you walked into Larson's office, there were already men preparing to pack items for auction. I suppose there were boxes and packing material already in the room. Oh, and labels. How am I doing?"

The younger woman lifted a finger. "There was only one man in the room."

"The man who broke into your home. The man you shot," Rose said with a tone of satisfaction she immediately regretted using.

Mrs. Miller murmured, "Yes."

"With someone watching you, you knew you couldn't simply walk out with the file. So, you picked up the trunk from somewhere close by—"

"It was on the desk. I'd stared at it a dozen times because it reminded me of a trunk I'd had as a child."

"For your doll," Rose said.

Mrs. Miller looked up at her with an incredulous expression. "How did you know that?"

"I had one, too."

The younger woman gave her a faint smile. "We seem to have a few things in common."

"More than you know. So, you slipped the papers under the lining. I suppose there was a letter opener nearby on the desk."

She nodded. "I was shaking so much because I was certain he'd wonder what I was doing so long at the desk."

"And the vase inside made a more appropriate gift than an empty unremarkable trunk," Rose said. "Why Mrs. VanderHelm?"

"It was something I decided in my panic at being discovered. I'd been working on some papers for one of her charities that morning. Her name and address were fresh on my mind, so I used it."

Rose finished again. "Because you couldn't risk sending anything to yourself without raising suspicion. The vase was merely a ruse, a possible if not probable gift for a woman like Mrs. VanderHelm. It might have gone differently if the vase had been valuable."

Rose drained her teacup and studied the delicate violet painted on the interior wall, no doubt rendered by a woman sitting in a stifling factory, earning barely enough to feed her children. She looked up at the woman across from her, a new generation of women daring to cross the lines of acceptable employment. "Mrs. Miller, why did you come to see me? Surely, not because of a prick of conscience. Why would you feel the need to confess to me, a stranger?"

Her chin raised, her gaze direct, she asked, "You have the trunk, don't you?"

It didn't sound like a question but a statement of fact. Rose returned her gaze with her own deliberate one. "If I did, why would that be of importance?" It was a silly game and Rose silently chastised herself for playing it, but she was curious to watch how the woman handled herself in an unsympathetic situation.

"You know why. I'm certain of it. You had too little evidence to lead you to conclude my father was being blackmailed."

Rose shook her head. "You are mistaken. I deduced that from an afternoon's study of three years of articles about trials in which your father served as prosecuting attorney. It took little more than an hour for each year of your father's cases to find a disturbing trend. What would make an attorney with such an outstanding record of convictions suddenly begin to lose them with such alarming regularity?"

"My father's a brilliant attorney," Mrs. Miller said defiantly, but her voice altered, lacking the fire of her previous statement.

"I'm quite certain of it, which is why the record is so telling. The natural question is why was he unable to apply that brilliance in the last five cases of his career?" Rose pulled from her pocket the folded papers and placed them on the table between them. She rested her fingers lightly on them and kept her gaze on Mrs. Miller.

The woman's lips drained of color as she pressed them into a tight line. "What are you going to do with them?"

"What were *you* going to do with them?"

The widow's trembling hands lay on the table, inches away from the papers. "Destroy them, of course!" She looked up from the papers, her eyes wide with alarm. "Surely, you won't give them to the police? You can't trust them."

"Unfortunately, I have to agree with you. Not all are tainted, but I think Mr. Larson had his fingers around the necks of a vast number of Denver citizens and public officials." Rose leaned forward and lowered her voice. "Do you know what information Larson had on your father?"

The woman sat back and dropped her hands into her lap. "It involved a partnership on a mining claim. They killed his partner. It was an accident, but Larson intimidated someone into implicating my father in his murder. It wasn't true, of course. If you knew my father . . . he's a gentleman, ruthless as an attorney, but he'd never have killed a man."

"You've never read these, have you?" She tapped her nail against her cup.

Mrs. Miller squeezed her eyes tight. "No. I don't think I want to. I just want them destroyed so no one else has to suffer like my father." Her voice trailed off.

"You need no more proof of your husband's murder than to know these papers exist. They marked your husband and his friend as targets just because they knew the papers existed."

The widow dropped her face into her hands.

Rose visualized Dr. Whitman's wrinkled brow, a warning she'd gone too far, and changed her tone. "As much as I admire your courage, you took a terrible risk. You've put your father's life and your own in danger." But she knew her own hypocrisy for declaring it. She and Casey were following down the same set of tracks, her sister on one rail, she on the other.

In their own way, each was taking risks to accomplish the same aim—justice—a goal worth any risk to achieve.

"What life?" A fire flamed again in the younger woman's eyes. "My father's been a mere shadow of his former self. You wouldn't know it to see him now. I hardly see the risk considering what he might gain if we destroyed those papers."

Rose allowed herself a rare smile. This was what she wanted to see in the woman—a resolve to see it through. "Then we need to visit Mr. Charles Kent and put the last piece of the puzzle in place."

Before she could explain, the hall phone rang. Mrs. Pennyworth must have been in the hall, just outside the room, listening in on their conversation. She called out, "Miss McKenzie, it's Detective Donahue. Needs to speak with you right away."

"Excuse me. I should take this call."

"Hello, detective. I'm pleased to hear from you. For a while, I thought we might only communicate through secret missives passed in the night."

There was a pause, then she heard him clear his throat. "I've just come back from the morgue."

"That's unpleasant," Rose said.

"Miss McKenzie, please be serious."

"I am. I've been there. It is unpleasant," Rose said.

"One of our patrolmen found the body of a man that matches the description that Mrs. Miller gave us of the intruder. Dr. Whitman told me she's with you?"

"That's good news, isn't it?"

"The man didn't die from the gunshot Mrs. Miller inflicted.

They had shot him."

Rose almost asked if he was sure but stopped before humiliating herself. Of course, the coroner would know what killed him. He wouldn't have been running with a shot through his cranium. After a heavy pause, she stated the obvious aloud. "Someone else is looking for . . ."

"Of course, there is."

"It is also why you've had your officers watching my house," she said.

A pause and then, "Yes, I posted a man to watch your house. They aren't stupid. If they didn't have it figured out before that it involved you, they do now. Mrs. Miller probably led them right to your door."

"Wait a minute. You said your men are watching the house. Not following me?" Rose asked, as the face of the man in the storefront window appeared as a perfect photograph in her mind's eye.

"I don't have the authority for that kind of surveillance." Detective Donahue's voice lowered, and she pictured him holding his hand, cupping the phone speaker. "Have you considered how much that information is worth? If you have the papers, you need to hand them over to me."

"Since you gave me your own information in such a clandestine fashion, then you obviously know handing over to the police anything I might have is unwise."

"I can see that I put them in the right hands." He sounded pleading now. "As long as they know you have them, you're putting yourself in unnecessary danger."

"Detective Donahue, you know it isn't you I distrust."

From the other side of the line, came the distinct sound of a heavy exhalation of breath. "What are you planning to do?"

"First of all. I'd like to know how you learned the thief was looking for papers."

Another pause, much longer stretched out before the detective answered, "I might have overheard a conversation between you and the doctor."

"You eavesdropped on us?" Rose felt the heat rise up her neck and her hair at the base of her skull tingled with it. "You were in the hospital garden. That was you."

A sound of swallowing came clear through the receiver. "Yes."

The acrid smell of smoke trumped her simmering anger. She spun to look toward the parlor. "I have to go."

Mrs. Miller stood before the fireplace and held the papers above a flaming match. In the seconds it took Rose to cross the room at a run, the bottom corner was aflame. "You can't do that!" She grabbed for the woman's hand, but as Mrs. Miller pulled away, the air fanned the flames upward. Rose threw both arms around the woman and with her full weight fell on her, a tackle that would have made her uncle cheer. It might have surpassed the one she'd made on the streetcar.

With the breath knocked from the younger woman, Rose tore the pages from the woman's fist. She yanked the small, hooked rug from in front of the hearth and used it to smother the flames. There'd be a recompense with Mrs. Pennyworth later.

Panting, Rose sat up with her back resting against the piano leg, sucking on her scorched fingertips.

Mrs. Miller rolled to her side and glared at Rose. "We must destroy them."

"We will, but not yet. Look at the last name on this paper." Rose passed it to her.

The younger woman blinked and sat up, reading the entry next to Charles Kent's name.

Rose nodded and took the paper back, folding it with the others. "We need to have a talk with your employer. I think his magnanimous attitude toward women in law careers may lack a certain veracity. Do you think you're up to it, Victoria?"

With an undeniable glint of steel in her eyes, the younger woman lifted her chin and nodded once.

Rose suppressed a cheer. Such women would change the course of the next century.

CHAPTER 24

When Rose and Mrs. Miller arrived at Charles Kent's office, the front door stood ajar. Rose turned to Victoria, putting a finger to her lips. She took two steps closer, listening for any sound from within. Nothing. Rose fumbled in her bag for the Smith and Wesson, and felt another stab of envy for Casey's habit of carrying her weapon in a holster. It might be time to reconsider her sleuthing wardrobe in favor of something more practical.

She pressed her fingers against the wood-paneled door and eased it open a few inches. Kent's secretary was not at her desk. Rose deduced, from the perfectly arranged items on the desk, that the secretary was not in the office, perhaps having left for the day.

Rose leaned close to Victoria's ear and whispered, "Stay here. I'm going in." She pointed to the lawyer's office at the end of the hall. "I know you can shoot." She handed her .32 to Victoria, who looked a little too pale. Recalling that the doctor had not approved her dismissal from the hospital, she wondered if it had been a mistake to bring her. "Are you all right?"

Victoria nodded and wiped her right palm on her skirt before settling the pistol in her hand. She gave Rose an odd smile and whispered, "I like it."

Rose shot her a quizzical look.

"Your pistol. I like it. It's lighter than the .38."

Rising on the balls of her feet, Rose approached the door, listening for sounds of movement. From within, she could make out a man's angry voice. Rose eased the door open until it met some resistance. On the floor, she saw a thick volume of *Black's Law* and beyond it a scattering of more reference books. She pushed the door farther.

Rose kneeled on the floor beside the overturned bookcase beside the lawyer. She studied him as he leafed through a book that had fallen there. It was an anomalous scene, with the man appearing to be searching for some specific passage amidst the ruin of his library. She scanned the room to assure herself no one else was there and pocketed the gun. "Mr. Kent? Are you injured?"

He lifted his head, a glazed look in his gray eyes as though he was seeing through her. "May I help you?"

Rose called out, "Victoria, you can come in." Navigating the disarray of books, she cleared a space with her foot and knelt in front of him. "Mr. Kent. I'm Rose McKenzie. Do you remember me?"

Upon entering the room, Victoria gave out a low cry. She shoved aside the books blocking her way and leaned over, laying her hand on the man's back. "Let me help you up."

THE CASE OF THE PECULIAR INHERITANCE

Rose righted the office chair while Victoria guided the lawyer to his seat.

"I'll get you some water," Victoria said.

His eyes focused again as he stared into his assistant's face. "Looks like I can't do much without you around." He gave out an unnatural laugh. "Foolish of me. Tried to reach a book on the top shelf. The whole thing came down on me."

"You're a very lucky man, Mr. Kent. They could have killed you," Rose said.

He laughed again. "Killed by the tools of his trade." His voice was growing stronger as he turned to look at Rose. "Of course, I know you, Miss McKenzie. How's your investigation coming?"

A trail of blood trickled from the corner of his mouth to his chin. He must have sensed it then and pulled a handkerchief from his pocket, dabbing at it. A painful-looking swelling beneath his right eye appeared more the result of a blow from a fist than a falling book.

"Here you are. Drink this." Victoria hovered protectively at the man's side until he'd drained the glass.

"Thank you, Mrs. Miller." His eyes locked on hers for a protracted moment. "Your father must be very proud of you." His voice lacked its usual confidence, as a nearly imperceptible quaver attached itself to the words "proud of you." He cast his eyes to his desk and frowned. "This is quite a mess."

"Mr. Kent," Rose started.

He searched for something as he pushed papers aside randomly.

"Mr. Kent. You didn't get those injuries trying to retrieve a book from the bookcase."

His hands trembled.

"Who did this to you?" Rose persisted.

"Miss McKenzie, I don't think Mr. Kent is in any—"

The lawyer grabbed for Victoria's hand. "I'm sorry. This wasn't supposed to happen. None of it."

Victoria looked on the verge of tears as she wrapped both her hands around his. "I'm the one who took advantage of you to get what I wanted. I used my position here to get into Mr. Larson's home. This wouldn't have happened to you if I hadn't—"

"You don't know what I did, do you?" Kent pulled back from her and ran a shaky hand through his hair.

"I think I do," Rose said as she lifted the volume of *Blackstone's Commentaries* from the chair she'd occupied on her first visit. She studied it for a moment before reverently placing it on the desk and taking a seat. "You knew exactly why Mrs. Miller wanted this position. In fact, if I were a woman who enjoyed gambling, I'd put down a sizeable wager that you arranged for her to work here."

Victoria gave her an incredulous look, then shook her head. "I'm the one who found out that Mr. Larson was his client." She turned to Kent. "I'm so sorry."

Kent kept his gaze fixed on his hands, fingers splayed out on the desk as though holding it in place.

Rose directed her next words to Victoria. "Are you certain of that? Isn't it possible someone told you Mr. Larson was a client of Mr. Kent's?"

The steel Victoria had shown earlier faded from her eyes as she searched her memory, questioning what she believed was true. She frowned then and took a step back from the attorney, staring at him as though she didn't know the man. "You knew. You . . ."

"You wanted exactly what I did," Kent said, as he slowly reanimated, drawing his hands to his lap and squaring his shoulders. "You wanted to get your hands on whatever Larson had on your father. Whatever had transformed him from a tenacious prosecuting attorney into the fearful man he is today."

"But why did you need me? Why me? Why not get them yourself?" Victoria asked, her confusion now turning to anger.

Rose explained, "Because Larson would never have trusted you, Mr. Kent. He had power over you but knew you were only good to him as long as those papers were not in your hands. You banked on the attractive Mrs. Miller to use her wiles to get Mr. Larson to brag about his illegal activities. You knew how driven she was to identify her husband's murderer and restore her father's good name."

"You used me!" Victoria said as she leaned across the desk, her face inches from Kent's.

Rose walked around the desk and stood to the side of the window, looking down on the street below. "Why don't you tell us about the man you hired to watch Mrs. Miller?"

"I didn't intend for this to turn violent. When I learned about the break-in, I told him I didn't need his services anymore. He laughed and said that it was fine because he had a better offer from someone else. Exactly what I was trying to avoid. Don't you see?

If I could get my hands on the papers, I would have destroyed them." He looked imploringly at Mrs. Miller. "Just as you would have. Do you know how much money unscrupulous people would pay for this information? As long as the papers exist, there will never be a fair trial in this city."

"So, I'm asking again, Mr. Kent. Do you know who hired the man who did this to you?" Rose remained at the window, waiting for his answer.

"I have my suspicions, but the gentleman had no reason to answer any of my questions. All he wanted was for me to answer his and tell him where the papers were," Kent said. "But I didn't know."

Rose turned from the window and asked, "Did he tell you he'd killed the man you sent to trail Mrs. Miller?"

His face paled. "Killed?"

"Shot in the head," Rose answered.

"My God!"

"But he didn't kill you. Is that because you told him what he wanted to know?"

"I'm worth more alive than dead. As long as they control that blackmailer's information, why kill me?" he said.

Rose knew this last answer was correct, but he hadn't answered the first question. "Did you tell him what he wanted to know?"

His face turned ashen as he met her gaze. "God help me. I told them about you."

Rose nodded and turned back to look at the street below. "Good. I was hoping you did." The man leaned casually against the building. He continued to feign interest in his newspaper. She allowed herself the smallest suggestion of a smile. "I need to use your telephone, Mr. Kent."

He waved a hand to the wall.

She rang the number, hoping it would be the detective who answered his phone and not a subordinate.

"Detective Donahue speaking."

"This is Rose McKenzie. Send one of your officers to Mr. Kent's office. He has vital information about the man found murdered today. At the least, I think he can provide a list of names."

"Miss McKenzie, are you there?" Detective Donahue asked.

"Yes, detective. Mrs. Miller is here as well. I think it would be wise to provide her with some protection for the next few hours. Can you do that?"

The detective lowered his voice. "You mustn't do this alone. What are you planning? Tell me."

"I have every intention of telling you. You're a pivotal element of my plan."

Rose left Victoria with both the pistol and strict instructions to wait for the police to arrive. Although she'd have felt better leaving the woman armed, she preferred the Smith and Wesson to any other gun she owned, and she reasoned she'd be needing it.

When she returned to the lobby of Kent's office building, the messenger boy who'd been so helpful on her first visit stood to the side of the glass door. He was focused on something with such intensity that he must not have heard her because he startled when she approached. He gave her an eager smile. "Good afternoon, Miss. Making deliveries without your bicycle today?"

"I didn't bring it with me."

He glanced to the street again and turned back with a frown just visible beneath his tousled hair. "You want me to flag down a cab for you?"

"It's such a pleasant afternoon. I think I'll walk."

He frowned, his look one of concern. "There's a man over there across the street. He was there when I came in and he hasn't left yet. He's been there at least a half hour."

"Forty-five minutes."

"Excuse me, Miss?"

"He's been there—" Rose glanced up at the wall clock above the elevator doors. "Forty-six, to be precise."

Interrupting any further discussion and with a lack of any clandestine subtlety, the police wagon pulled up to the curb. The young deliveryman stepped outside, giving Rose the opportunity to slip behind him.

After a block of walking at her normal quick pace, she stole a glance over her shoulder, gratified to see the man keeping pace. If her plan was to succeed, she wouldn't want him to fall behind.

CHAPTER 25

Mrs. Pennyworth's eyes narrowed as she considered Rose's generous offer. "You're giving me the night off." The woman's lips compressed, giving Rose the impression that the housekeeper had transformed into a tightly sealed package. "To visit my sister in Fort Collins." She folded her arms across her chest, as if, for good measure, she'd tied her package with string. "You even bought me a ticket."

Rose said casually, "Yes. Didn't you mention just last week that you were overdue for a visit with your sister?"

The woman remained in her rigid stance, her chest rising and falling as an indication she was breathing.

"Besides, I forgot your birthday last month, didn't I? Consider this a belated present."

"You don't give presents," Mrs. Pennyworth said flatly.

Rose considered this for a moment, saying with confidence, "Of course, I give presents. I'm sure you're mistaken."

"Nope."

"Well, you're definitely overdue for one," Rose said cheerfully and pulled the train ticket from her skirt pocket, slapping it on the table between them.

"What's going on?" Mrs. Pennyworth asked, with an unmistakable tone of suspicion. "What are you up to, Miss Rose? Does this have anything to do with the man that's been skulking around behind the neighbor's hydrangea bushes? A crook would do a better job of hiding himself. In fact, I could do a better job."

While the housekeeper's eyes remained little more than slits, Rose felt her own widen. "There's a man behind the bushes?"

"You know there is. You might not notice if I served you green eggs for your breakfast, but you'd not miss seeing a man skulking in the bushes."

"Oh, the police officer? Yes. Um. You know how zealous Detective Donahue can be. He sent the officer over to watch the house until I resolve the case. You see? You shouldn't worry." Rose imagined her tone to be light and nonchalant, but judging from the housekeeper's skeptical expression, she remained unconvinced.

Mrs. Pennyworth rocked forward on her toes, whispering, "This has to do with those three break-ins. Now, don't look surprised. It's not like I'm blind and can't read all the details written on that board of yours upstairs for anyone to see. So, it was in the trunk, wasn't it? I knew it."

Rose refused to see her plans derailed by her housekeeper. "I think a brief trip will be good for you."

"I know you're up to something, and I'd bet my week's pay that it's risky."

It took three quarters of an hour to get Mrs. Pennyworth out of the house and into the cab. As Rose waved her off, she breathed out a heavy sigh of relief and turned her thoughts back to what she must prepare. The first would be a newsworthy telephone call.

Before she reached the hall phone, its bell rang impatiently. Rose answered, "Hello, this is Miss McKenzie."

"Rose, what are you up to?" the male voice demanded.

She pulled the phone a few inches from her ear and composed herself before responding to the now-familiar question. "Dr. Whitman, how nice of you to call."

A loud expulsion of breath assaulted her ear. "I wish you wouldn't make light of this. Detective Donahue just told me about the murdered man. He told me you were planning something to trap the killer? Tell me that's not what you're doing."

"That's not what I'm doing," Rose said obediently.

"You're lying, Rose McKenzie. If I were there, I'd see that nose of yours red as a beacon."

Rose glanced in the hall mirror. She touched the tip of her nose, turning an unattractive shade of red.

"I'm coming over. Don't stop me." A pause followed by a crackling of static. "You aren't going to try to stop me?"

"No," she said.

Another pause, followed by more static. Seconds later. "Why aren't you trying to stop me?"

"Might I simply enjoy your company?" Rose asked, as she glanced in the mirror at the tip of her nose.

The pause from the other end of the line stretched into a full minute. "I'm leaving immediately. Please do nothing foolish, Rose. At least, wait until I'm there before you do."

"Goodbye, Dr. Whitman." Rose bit down on her lower lip and hung up the receiver. Despite what the doctor and her housekeeper said about her taking unnecessary risks, she wasn't like her sister, who wouldn't hesitate to leap from one train car to another in pursuit of a miscreant. She was Rose, the one who carefully calculated her odds when a case called for some element of risk. The doctor might improve her odds or at least pick up the pieces if things went badly.

She lifted the receiver again and made the call to Mrs. VanderHelm.

"That's right. I found something valuable, after all. As you suspected, it was not the vase," Rose said.

"I'm so pleased to hear it. When you come tomorrow, we'll have tea and you can tell me all the details," Mrs. VanderHelm said. "Oh, and you can ask your friend, Dr. Whitman, to join us."

Rose added, "Please remember to tell Miss Finnegan and Mrs. Haycraft the news. I'm sure they'll rest better knowing they're safe from any further break-ins."

"I'll do that immediately. Thank you, Miss McKenzie. You've done an excellent job. I will definitely let my friends know of your services. Heaven forbid, they should need your help, I will tell them straight away to get in touch with you."

"Thank you, Mrs. VanderHelm."

Rose glanced in the mirror a third time. Her nose appeared only slightly pinker but not red. With pursed lips, she considered her reflection for a moment, taking in the inappropriateness of her attire. She needed something to allow more freedom of movement. The corset must go and perhaps a split skirt. A holster would be nice.

Her pulse quickened with a glance at the hall wall clock. Sunset was little more than an hour away. As she ran up the staircase, she reviewed her mental checklist. She could do this, if the facts she'd gathered also proved her suppositions. That dangerous knife-edge of speculation lifted tiny hairs along her neck.

Rose took in a rare but pleasantly deep breath as she removed her corset and threw it on the bed. She pulled from the closet clothing her sister had persuaded her to purchase when she'd last visited. After giving her reflection a cursory glance, she darted from the bedroom and ran upstairs to the attic.

Rose found the doll trunks exactly where Casey had stashed them under the eaves. She ran her fingers along the lid of her own. A warm rush of emotion washed over her as she held the small chest on her lap. Even before opening the lid fully, the scent of lavender wafted from the interior. Caroline's glass eyes stared up at hers, open and accepting. But they had always been that way, would always be that way, with carefully painted amber lines radiating from black pupils. The doll's hands, proportionally too small for its body, were open as though asking for a hug. Rose touched one finger to the doll's blond hair, the ragged curls shorn by Casey's hand.

A loud bang brought her back to the moment. She glanced over her shoulder to the attic doorway, listening. Colorado winds, as unpredictable and sudden as its violent thunderstorms, whipped branches against house exterior. Rose tucked Caroline back into her trunk and closed the lid before pulling Casey's trunk to her.

Unlike Caroline, Casey's doll had kept her raven locks, although showing the effects of too often being combed and coifed in a myriad of styles. Rose carefully lifted the doll from atop her bed of frocks, some handmade from embroidered handkerchiefs and scraps of outgrown dresses, a few store-bought. As though she might bruise with rough handling, Rose lay the doll in the folds of her skirt.

With less care, she removed the dresses and petticoats, releasing an odor of mildew. Rose frowned. This was no place for old friends to live out their years. With the trunk emptied, she peered in at the fabric liner. As she had with Larson's trunk, she ran her fingers along the edges until she found the slit made over fifteen years ago. She probed the space between the liner and the wood with her nail. Something smooth met her finger. With a slight tug, the emerald-green ribbon appeared. Lost to her all these years, the memory was as fresh as though having happened only yesterday. She held the ribbon up to the afternoon light streaming from the dormer window. The color hadn't faded, still as bright as when she'd last worn it to hold back her hair that day in May when a boy had pressed his lips to her cheek.

A branch struck the window, and Rose jumped. It was time. She pulled back her hair, tying it with the green ribbon. "I'll be back and give you both a proper home when I'm done." Then, emptying both trunks of

THE CASE OF THE PECULIAR INHERITANCE

their clothing and dolls, she stacked the boxes in her arms and took the stairs back to her study. A few more items remained on her list before her visitors arrived.

CHAPTER 26

Rose focused on the scale's numbers. When the balance arm stilled, she let out the breath she'd been holding for the past few seconds. She took another breath and held it as she poured the contents into the pan. "All right, Sergeant. I'm confident in the ratio." She glanced down at the hound sitting beneath the worktable. "At least, I'm just as confident as the last time plus a little more."

"We all know how well that went."

Her spoon dropped to the floor with a clatter. "Dr. Whitman! You should have announced yourself."

"I did. Why was your front door unlocked?"

"Was? Did you lock it?"

He regarded her for a moment, then left and returned soon after. "Let me start over. Do you know your front door is unlocked?"

"Maybe."

"You *are* up to something."

There was no ignoring the doctor's reproving tone, so similar to her housekeeper's. "What exactly does that mean? Up to something. As long as a person is breathing, they are up to something. It's a fact of nature," Rose said.

"You know what I mean. I have this dreadful feeling that you're deliberately luring this killer to your home. Tell me I'm wrong."

Rose opened her mouth to answer.

"No, don't answer that." He shook his head rather violently. "How can I talk you out of this?"

She opened her mouth.

"No, don't answer that. I know there's no hope of that." He paced the length of her worktable.

Rose grabbed his sleeve as he passed behind her. "Please, be careful. Don't bump the table."

He spun on her, opened his mouth, and snapped it shut again.

Rose walked to the basin, carefully washed her hands, walked around the table, and faced him. "Look, I invited you to join me. I believe that in doing so, I've reduced the risk."

He squeezed his eyes shut, whispering, "You're impossible."

"But you still like me," Rose said.

He lifted an eyebrow, revealing a wolfish gleam in his eye as he took a step toward her.

With a sudden gust of wind, the window rattled violently, startling them both, and theatrically shattering Dr. Whitman's opportunity for a romantic moment.

"I hope this storm doesn't discourage my guest," Rose said as she skirted the worktable to the chalkboard. She scrubbed her notes from the board with a rag she took from the table.

"I thought Detective Donahue had a man on surveillance outside. I didn't see anyone when I got here." Dr. Whitman crossed to the window with a view to the street.

"He's behind the hydrangeas."

"Ah. Undercover."

Rose picked up a new stick of chalk and wrote the name in large letters complete with flourishes on either end. **Calvin Hollingsworth.** The embellishment suited the name.

"Is this the man we're expecting to come and murder you?"

She scowled. "I may need to ask you to leave if you're going to continue to be unpleasant. I'm not expecting the man to murder either of us."

The windows rattled again. This time the wind beat at them with a flurry of hail. Just as Rose was mentally calculating the force required to break a window, the sound of shattering glass rose above the fury of the storm. "Quick!" Rose grabbed Sergeant's collar and motioned for the doctor to follow.

She pushed aside the Brontë book and pulled the lever for the door to open into her hidden room beneath the eaves. With no time for an explanation, she shoved both the dog and the doctor inside. Before pulling the door closed, she whispered, "There's a small hole drilled into the door. See it? Good. If things don't go as planned, I'm sure you're clever enough to do something quite brave." Before the doctor could protest, she closed the door and hurried to position herself between the chalkboard and the laboratory table. In front of her, the three small trunks sat in a straight row, looking remarkably similar in size and shape.

THE CASE OF THE PECULIAR INHERITANCE

From the sound of the man's heavy steps thundering on the stairs, she hoped the intruder believed the house to be empty. She further counted on the simple fact that the darkened house gave her the advantage over the man who would have to feel his way about. Without moonlight to assist him, it would impede his ability to search the house. But she had no intention of allowing the man to ransack her home. She lit the oil lamp on the worktable.

The footsteps stopped at the top landing.

"You'll find me in here," Rose said.

It was as if the man's thoughts were being fed through electric wires of a telephone—alarm, confusion, cursing of the most vulgar type. The footsteps resumed, approaching the door with a measure of caution. The flat face with square jaw illuminated by the oil lamp was not that of the individual she expected.

Annoyed, Rose watched the man step farther into the room. "Mr. McAllister, how interesting to see you again. Are you here to make me an offer? I believe that's how it's done."

"I know what you found. I'd like to have it now," the man said, sounding both irritated and confident. "You'll never get the price for it I can. I know what information like that is worth, and I know those that would pay for it. So, why don't I make you a deal. Fifty percent could mean quite a nice return on your investment."

"I'm not planning to invest in any part of extortion," Rose said, feeling heat rise in her belly.

"I'm talking about investing in your insurance to stay alive." McAllister gave her a crooked smile. "Don't worry. I'm not a violent man. I just know there are men out there that wouldn't hesitate to kill for the information you're holding. As I see it, I'm your best option."

"You think they'll not do the same to you once they know you have it? What makes you immune to their reprisals, Mr. McAllister?"

Even in the low light, Rose detected a shadow of doubt pass over the man's face. He crossed the space between the door and the table. "I want the papers, Miss McKenzie."

"I'm curious. How did you know what people were searching for?"

"There weren't many in this town who didn't know what the man was doing. Anyone with half a brain. No one is lucky enough to escape jail time as many times as he did."

Rose recognized the truth of what he'd said. "So, why didn't anyone try to get their hands on them before he died? Why wait?"

"For one reason. Anyone who ever tried ended up dead. Now, there's a case for a detective. No one knew, but after a half-dozen intruders ended up in the Denver morgue, no one else attempted it. Personally, I think it was his housekeeper. Did you meet her? That's one woman I wouldn't want to run into in a dark room. I'm not even sure she's human. I gotta hand it to that young woman, Mrs. Miller. She got them right out from under Brunhilde's nose."

"With all you've just told me, about the violent men, the vindictive housekeeper, and the intensity of the search for these documents, you're willing to put your life at risk as a broker?

What makes you believe they'll be willing to negotiate?"

McAllister's facial confidence took a downward turn. He glanced down at the small trunks arranged in front of him. "What is this? A shell game?" He studied the trunks, settling on the middle one. "This is the one in the house, wasn't it?" He gave a snort. "I searched everywhere."

He placed both hands on the lid and jerked it open. A sudden flash of blinding light illuminated every startled feature of the man's face. White smoke swirled about the table, engulfing the man and sending him into fits of coughing. In the next moment, Dr. Whitman burst from the room, grabbed him, and threw him to the ground.

Rose might have completely missed the doctor's tackle if she hadn't closed her eyes right at the moment of the flash. Perhaps not as good as her own tackle but adequate for the job. Rose pulled her gun from her pocket and kept it leveled on McAllister as another spasm of coughing overcame him.

"Here." Rose handed the doctor her leather belt. "Bind his hands with this." She reached over and snatched the rag from her table and gagged the man. "Can you use your belt for his feet?"

Dr. Whitman threw her a puzzled glance. "Why don't we just get the attention of the useless police officer hiding in the hydrangea bush?"

"Because there isn't time."

"What do you mean?"

"This isn't Hollingsworth. That means he's still coming."

CHAPTER 27

Dr. Whitman stood looking understandably confused, and from the line of disapproval deepening on his broad forehead, he was even more irritated by her explanation. But with no time to explain, she took McAllister's arm and imploringly looked over at the doctor. "Help me move him. Sergeant will guard him for us."

"Why?"

"Why shouldn't Sergeant help us?"

Uncharacteristically, the doctor raised his voice. "No! I wasn't talking about Sergeant. Why should we move the man?"

"Isn't it obvious? Hollingsworth will be here any minute, and he can't find us apprehending random felons. He mustn't view me as a threat. I want him to believe he's in complete control of the situation. I want him confident, even cocky."

Apparently, seeing little recourse, the doctor took the man's other arm and together they dragged him into the room where they propped him against the wall under the sloping ceiling. Rose patted Sergeant on the head and rewarded him with one of Mrs.

Pennyworth's biscuits she'd stashed in her pocket. "Keep the wicked man quiet."

Sergeant let out a low growl, plopping himself down across the man's feet.

Rose backed to the door and turned to the doctor with another look of unspoken appeal.

"What? You want me to stay in here again? No! I'm absolutely not going to stay in here with your dog while you face down whoever it is who shows up next." The doctor folded his arms defiantly. "A man has his pride." The defiance didn't communicate well as his height required him to bend his head at an acute angle to avoid the low ceiling.

Rose took a precious moment to ponder the options in light of their new circumstances. Those circumstances now required a modicum of compromise. "Then help me set up a new trap."

The doctor pulled the door closed behind him while Rose hurried back to the worktable. White smoke still lingered in the room. She lifted the sash just enough to send the smoke in swirling tendrils to the ceiling.

"What now?" the doctor asked.

Rose surveyed the ruined interior of Larson's trunk, scorched and soot-covered. She had no time to reset the flash pan. Besides, the recent burn marks along the cover would arouse suspicion.

Dr. Whitman leaned over the trunk and asked, "How did you ignite the magnesium?"

Rose lifted a cylinder with small wires extending from it. "It's a dry cell battery, a useful device invented by Mr. Cowen. I wrote to him when I read about his patent for a safer method he'd devised for photographers. Brilliant, isn't it?"

"Hmm. I'm relieved I'm not trying to patch your face back together right now. You will not try to make another one, right?"

"I was, but there isn't time. We must improvise."

He started to speak when Rose put up her finger to his lips. "Listen," she whispered.

Light footsteps tread upon the wood floorboards, shuffling from the parlor to the dining room and farther down the hall and into the kitchen. Rose gestured frantically to the room behind the bookcase.

The doctor emphatically shook his head. He then gestured for her to go inside the room, to which she replied with an exaggerated mouthing of the word "no."

They both turned when the footsteps started up the stairs. Rose whispered into the doctor's ear, "We'll both go in."

Pulling the doctor into the room with both the hound and the auctioneer sitting beneath the desk wasn't easy. The space was comfortable enough for Rose and her dog, but with the added bodies, there was scarce room to maneuver. Rose closed the door behind them and put her eye up to the small hole into the larger room, giving her only a wedge-shaped view of the room.

Footsteps stopped at the door to the lab, then crept to the table before Rose saw his face. The man she'd recognized, the foxlike face reflected in the store window, the man she'd seen but once years before, glanced about the room. Randall Hollingsworth would be good at what he did and waste no time, a true professional and a protege of Allan Pinkerton.

If he examined the trunks, his back would be to her hiding place and she might surprise him. She reached into her pocket for the .32. In extracting it, she drove her elbow into the doctor's stomach. The sharp expulsion of breath, his lungs' natural response to the blow, escaped his lips with a muffled *oof*, enough to make Hollingsworth turn. The man froze, his gaze sweeping the wall of bookcases once, then twice.

Rose held her breath, cautioning the doctor by bringing a finger to her lips.

Hollingsworth's posture relaxed, and he stepped to the table, drawn to the trunks resting there.

The doctor leaned close to whisper in her ear. "Let me see."

Rose relinquished her position and allowed him access to the view. While he pressed his eye to the opening, Rose checked her gun in the dim light from the dormer window. Shooting the man did not factor into her original plan, but if she must, she would. Her uncle had taught her early in life to prepare for plans to go wrong, even the most carefully crafted ones. Never assume rescue would come from any source, aside from what your own wits devised.

Dr. Whitman hissed out of the corner of his mouth, "Who is that?"

"That's the man I was expecting." She dropped the weapon to her side.

"Not him. Her! The woman standing between this peephole and the man at the table. That's the back of a woman's head I'm seeing, something I'd surely recognize."

Rose pushed him aside and pressed her eye to the hole. "Blast!" She hissed and turned to the doctor, their noses nearly touching. "It's Victoria Miller."

Dr. Whitman peered through the opening again. "She has a gun! When did every woman start carrying a gun? Have they become a fashion accessory?" He must have felt the gun pressing against his thigh because he backed a few inches away. He looked down at the weapon in her hand, frowning. "Case in point." He looked through the hole again, whispering, "Why is she here?"

"Revenge, I imagine. She knew I was going to lure the man here."

Victoria's voice was low and steady, muffled by the door between them. "You're the one, aren't you?"

Rose pushed Dr. Whitman out of her way and watched through the hole, still unable to see more than the back of the woman's head. She considered whispering loud enough for Victoria to hear her, but the possibility of the woman's startled reaction giving away their hiding place was too great.

"Well, I am one, Mrs. Miller. I'm the one who came for Larson's documents, if that's what you mean. Do you have them? You didn't before, but I suspect Miss McKenzie gave them to you."

"You're the one responsible for my husband's death." Her voice trembled with anger. "Larson sent you to silence him."

"Oh, that."

Rose stiffened at the offhand tone, enough to make her want

to shoot him herself. She could only imagine how it stoked the rage boiling in Victoria.

"Yes, *that*!"

Victoria moved to the right and took two steps closer to the man, granting Rose a view of the complete scene. Like a shoot-out from one of her western adventure stories, each held a gun leveled at the other. It would have been helpful to know Mrs. Miller's skill with the weapon. Unlikely, she would have had any experience under such pressure.

Rose pushed the door open a scant inch. Dr. Whitman lay his hand on her shoulder. An unspoken, but clearly expressed message passed between them. Rose reached up with her free hand and gave him an answering pat.

Hollingsworth might also have been evaluating the woman's skill with the .38 because he kept her talking, buying some time for himself to maneuver into a better position as well. "It was business. Larson couldn't afford the adverse publicity. There was a court case pending against him, and he had to ensure his charitable reputation exceeded any concerns of impropriety in his business dealings."

Rose stepped through the door, insinuating herself into the shadows.

"How dreadful for Mr. Larson," Victoria sneered. "How inconvenient for him!"

Hollingsworth shrugged. "Like I said, business."

Rose spoke from the shadows. "It's even worse than you suggest, Mr. Hollingsworth. You were the detective who Larson hired to find the dirt, every bit of scandalous possibility that he could use as occasion required."

Both Victoria and Hollingsworth swung their heads in her direction.

With her eyes focused on Hollingsworth, Rose spoke to Victoria. "We have evidence now. We can turn him over to the authorities. Let me handle this."

Hollingsworth laughed. "You're going to handle it, Miss McKenzie, a woman who couldn't make the cut for the Pinkertons?"

Hair prickled along Rose's neck as heat rose to her ears. She took a steadying breath. "Considering the likes of you who once numbered with the best of Mr. Pinkerton's agents, I think it was providential that I failed. Look at you now—a common criminal."

As impassive as he appeared, something in the stiffening of his jaw suggested otherwise. "Oh, I'm far from common, Miss McKenzie. I have talents others could only dream of acquiring. I know things."

Knowledge is power. There it was again, the motivation and the man who wanted it most standing before her. He inched closer to Victoria.

The move did not go unnoticed. Rose took a step closer to Victoria and the end of the table. "If you were the one who gathered the information, why would you need the file? Don't you have all you need to continue the empire your boss constructed?" Rose asked.

Something she'd said stung. Any aplomb faded from his earlier self-confidence as he muttered a curse. "The crook fired me two years ago. Gave me a measly three thousand dollars and told me to disappear." He gave a mirthless laugh. "No one treats me that way."

"But if he treated you that way, why didn't you use your persuasive talents on him?" Rose took another step right. "Wouldn't you have had opportunities to break-in and steal them yourself?" She watched Victoria's arm sag. The .38 had to be difficult for her to hold steady, certainly heavier than Rose's snub-nose pistol. She knew Hollingsworth noticed the same thing as he stalled for time.

The man swung his head from Victoria to Rose. "You don't know how fortified that house was."

"I would imagine a man of your *talents* had something to do with that. It must have stung to know you'd locked yourself out of access to your lucrative blackmailing scheme. Maybe you were a little too good at your job of protecting your boss."

Victoria stepped back and extended her arm, reaching up with her other hand to steady the gun. "This is pointless! I don't care about your sad story. I care about making things right for my husband and father." Victoria's shrill voice caused Rose concern. Teetering on the knife-edge of reason might tip the scale in Hollingsworth's favor.

Everything the woman experienced in that moment hit Rose like a bolt of electricity, connecting her viscerally to the woman's rage and grief. Her suffering resembled her own outrage at deferred justice. So all-consuming was that desire for restitution that the normal process of grief stalled in stages like denial and anger. Part of Rose wanted Victoria to find some sense of release in the man responsible for killing her husband but not the rational part of her brain.

Victoria's voice carried the weight of her grief, words thrown like daggers at the man who'd robbed her of all she held dear. "Why should you continue to even breath when my husband never saw his twentieth birthday? You deserve to die."

Rose felt the sting of tears and blinked furiously. This was no time for empathy, pulling up dark murderous desires she'd harbored for years. She had exacted revenge a thousand times in a thousand ways in her imagination. She forced a calm into her voice, saying, "Victoria, this won't bring him back. Nothing will change if you kill him, not the injustice or the pain."

Victoria took a step closer to Hollingsworth. "I can't trust the courts to bring him to justice. I can't!"

Hollingsworth lifted his revolver, a nearly imperceptible degree. It was enough justification for Rose.

Rose fired the .32, and Hollingsworth collapsed to the floor, screaming in pain. Her aim had been true, and she felt certain the doctor would concur that his kneecap would never function as it once had.

As both the doctor and the hound exploded from the open door, Sergeant skirted Rose and dove under the table. So intent on defending his mistress, he didn't heed Rose's command to stop.

Hollingsworth lifted his hand, still gripping the gun and aimed at the dog. Rose knew in that instant she had no clear shot without the probability of hitting Sergeant.

From the corner of her eye, she watched as Dr. Whitman grabbed Victoria's arm and pulled her out of range. Victoria struggled to break free, brandishing her gun dangerously close to the doctor's chest.

A shot rang out.

The bullet that struck Hollingsworth's gun hand came from neither Rose nor Victoria's weapon but from the .45 Colt in Mrs. Pennyworth's hand.

With all eyes turning on the housekeeper, she lowered her Peacemaker and returned their wide-eyed astonishment by pursing her lips and saying, "Couldn't let him shoot the dog, could I?"

Rose knew she'd never write a better climactic scene than this one.

CHAPTER 28

With the chaotic atmosphere in the room, Mrs. Miller's sobs, Hollingsworth's pathetic whimpering, and the hound baying at his successful attack on the perpetrator, no one noticed Detective Donahue entering the room along with the slim young man he dragged in with him.

The detective cleared his throat, and yelled, "For the love of Mike, what is going on?"

Rose recovered her composure and answered the detective's question. "We have your killer. Calvin Hollingsworth over there, the one screaming. He worked for Mr. Larson and decided he would try to continue the man's extortion and blackmail over Denver."

The detective looked appraisingly at Hollingsworth while taking in the gun still in Rose's hand. He gestured to the Smith and Wesson. "Was that the gun used?"

Rose threw a quick glance at her housekeeper, whose calm was admirable, considering the circumstances. "One."

Detective Donahue squinted at her. "One?"

The young man still in the detective's grip tipped his hat to

Rose, giving her an uncertain smile. "Hello, Miss Winchester. Sorry, it took me so long to come. The storm made a bit of a mess. Had to leg it here through some flooded streets."

Detective Donahue stared at the young reporter and then back to Rose, uncomprehending. "Miss Winchester?"

"I'll explain later." Rose considered the grip with which Detective Donahue held the young man and asked, "Why are you holding on to Mr. O'Brien in that manner?"

The detective turned a baffled expression to Rose. "Found him in your entry downstairs. Told me you'd called him late this afternoon and asked him to come over for an exclusive story."

"I did, in fact."

"*Denver Evening Post*. Told you," the reporter said with a supercilious grin.

After a moment of hesitation that included an exchange of some unbecoming language, the detective released his hold on the man and turned his attention back to the other members in the room. "Was anyone else injured?"

"I am grateful to say no other injuries were inflicted." Rose folded her arms, studying the police officer. "To be honest, we rather expected a little more help from your officer hiding in the bushes."

Donahue ran a hand down the front of his jacket, looking somewhat uncomfortable. "There were two of them out there. By the time I was free to join them, someone had rendered both men unconscious. I was just tending to them when I heard the shots. Came inside and found this man lurking in the dark."

"I was not lurking. I was trying not to bruise my shins on the furniture. It's dark down there," Mr. O'Brien said.

The detective looked around as though expecting backup. Seeing none he asked, "I need to use your telephone to call the station. Looks like the man might need an ambulance."

Mrs. Pennyworth patted Donahue's back. "I'll go downstairs with you, detective. Show you the phone. Then, I'll brew a pot of my special tea for everyone." She threw a thumb toward Hollingsworth. "Except him."

"Thank you, Mrs. Pennyworth," the detective said, while offering her his arm. "I'm sorry this happened. This must have been a frightening ordeal for you."

Mrs. Pennyworth rolled her eyes dramatically. "Oh, it was terrifying." She extended her hand and held it for the detective to see. "Look! I'm still trembling."

Rose would need to have a long chat with her housekeeper. She'd neglected to mention a few of her nonculinary skills on her resume. "Sergeant, come here." Rose kneeled before the dog and rewarded him with a good head scrubbing. "You did very well, boy. But that was risky of you."

Mr. O'Brien positioned himself close to the fallen Hollingsworth, already scribbling notes before he'd interviewed a single witness. He caught Rose watching him and grinned. "You aren't really a writer, are you?"

She might have waited a moment too long before answering. "I'm a detective, Mr. O'Brien." Rose helped Victoria to her feet and into the wing chair by the corner stove. "This story has a wider scope than you think. I believe it will undoubtedly get you that byline you're after," Rose said, fighting the smugness threatening to seep into her voice. "Why don't you bring over one of those lab stools and sit here beside Mrs. Miller."

While Mr. O'Brien obliged, Rose pulled over another chair, creating an intimate semi-circle around the stove. "Dr. Whitman, is your patient able to stand?"

"Not without some pain."

"Unfortunate, but necessary. I have a chair for him near the stove."

Nearly giddy, the reporter chuckled while scribbling on his pad.

Rose leaned over and asked Victoria, "Are you willing to answer a few questions from this reporter?" She held Victoria's dull eyes with hers, making sure the young widow comprehended what she was asking of her. The woman would have to dig deep for some of the steel she'd displayed earlier. "We need to make it clear to the public that Larson's blackmailing enterprise is over. You can help me do that by telling your story to the press. Do you understand, Victoria? Those who might think they can continue what Larson started must know it's finished."

Victoria stared at her for an uneasy moment, and Rose feared she had slipped into shock. But clarity returned to the young woman's eyes, and she nodded. "Yes. I'm tired of fighting this battle alone."

The reporter frowned, his attitude shifting from one of curiosity to keen interest. "What battle, Mrs. Miller? I'm certain my readers will want to know your story."

Rose left the room to make her way to the stair landing, where she saw the detective hang up the receiver of the phone in the entry below her. "Detective Donahue, please come upstairs? I need your assistance."

The officer started for the stairs, but when Mrs. Pennyworth arrived at the bottom step at the same moment carrying her pot of tea and teacups, he took the tray from her hands and followed her up the stairs.

"Here you go, Mrs. Miller," Mrs. Pennyworth said with the same authority she'd often heard in the doctor's tone, as though her tea was a tonic as good as any medicine. Rose stopped her with a touch of a finger on the housekeeper's sleeve.

"I'd like you to stay, too, Mrs. Pennyworth," Rose said.

Hollingsworth wore an ominous expression. His pain left him speechless, but what he communicated with his eyes was foul enough to pollute the air.

Still looking ill at ease, Detective Donahue stood rigidly behind Hollingsworth's chair, ensuring the man did not escape. With the quantity of blood staining Rose's carpet, the ex-Pinkerton would be hard-pressed to muster the strength to make it halfway to the door.

The assembled members of the recent drama looked at each other with a mixture of awkwardness and venomous hatred until Rose realized they were waiting for her to proceed. "Aside from our reporter here, the rest of us know that all of this is a result of Mr. Randall Larson's extensive blackmail file on Denver's businessmen and officers of the law." The elevation of the reporter's eyes from his notebook to her, followed by the rapid scratching of his pencil across the paper, satisfied Rose.

"The file was the motivation for three break-ins, two assaults, and one murder," she explained.

Grinning like a schoolboy, Mr. O'Brien wagged his head, writing notes like a human dynamo.

"Mr. Hollingsworth not only killed the man hired by Mr. Kent to secure the file, but he is, by his own confession, guilty of involvement in at least one other murder, Mrs. Miller's husband. With some detective work by Denver's police force, I imagine further charges will come now that our city's legal counsels are out from under the threats posed by Mr. Larson's accumulated information."

Mrs. Pennyworth leaned over and whispered, "Miss McKenzie, is this going to take much longer? I've got tarts in the oven."

"You can leave if you must," Rose said irritably.

"Don't have to, I suppose. Shame, though. I used the last of the cherries."

"Oh, for goodness' sake, Mrs. Pennyworth. Go see to your tarts."

Mrs. Pennyworth left from the room, and for some reason, the hound followed her.

Hollingsworth groaned, "Officer, I've lost a lot of blood. I need a doctor. Have you called for one?"

"I *am* a doctor," Dr. Whitman said, his tone giving evidence of his offense.

"I called an ambulance. Be quiet." Detective Donahue smacked the back of Hollingsworth's head and said curtly, "Let the woman finish."

"Ouch! What's the point of me listening to this?" Hollingsworth growled.

"The point is, you have nowhere else to go except jail," the detective said. "If I were you, I wouldn't be in a hurry to get there."

Hollingsworth smirked. "I still know things. I still have information about the judges in this city that they wouldn't like made public." He tapped his temple. "All of it up here."

"We have eyewitnesses to your involvement with Larson's intimidations and even a confession of murder," Rose said. "I agree with Detective Donahue. I'm not sure being placed behind bars will be a healthy place for you. You've made a prodigious number of enemies."

Hollingsworth slouched in his chair, shooting her a venomous look.

"Where are the papers, Miss McKenzie?" Victoria asked apprehensively. "You still have them, don't you?"

"Of course, I have them." Rose would have preferred someone ask her where she'd hidden them, but even after a long pause, no one granted her the satisfaction of inquiring. She sighed and turned back to the bookcase and the open door to her writing room. It was such a great hiding place, too. In plain view, if someone had conducted a thorough search, which they hadn't.

THE CASE OF THE PECULIAR INHERITANCE

A movement from the darkened corner of the room caught Rose's attention. "Mr. McAllister! We forgot you were here."

The detective slipped into the cramped room along with Dr. Whitman and the reporter behind them.

"Who's that?" the reporter and the detective asked in unison.

Mr. McAllister mumbled.

"Help me get him out of here," Detective Donahue said to the reporter.

Rose frowned.

"What is it?" Dr. Whitman asked.

"No one saw where I'd hidden the blackmail papers."

"Where did you hide them, Miss McKenzie?" the doctor asked.

She didn't like his tone, as though he were placating her. Turning to her writing desk, Rose withdrew Larson's papers from the typewriter. "Here."

"Brilliant," he said flatly, with not the slightest sign of surprise.

Rose brushed past him and back into the larger room. "Mrs. Miller, would you care to light the fire in the stove? It's a little chilly in here. I believe that Mrs. Pennyworth has placed kindling inside as she usually does."

Mrs. Miller looked at her strangely, then seeing the papers in her hand, rose quickly and did as she was bid.

"There were two types of people who wanted to get their hands on these papers. Those like Mr. Hollingsworth and Mr. McAllister, who would use them to gain financially." Rose noticed the gag she'd tied around the auctioneer's mouth remained in place. She saw no reason to bring it to anyone's attention and proceeded. "And those who wished to destroy them, like Mrs. Miller."

"The sad fact facing us is that there are many others outside this room who would want them for personal gain. That's why you are here, Mr. O'Brien." She met the reporter's eager expression. "You and the detective here must be our witnesses."

Rose took the three steps to where Mrs. Miller stood. "You don't know what's on this page, but you do not need to know. I think you should have the privilege of burning the first one." She placed a single piece of paper into the woman's shaking hand.

Tears welling in her eyes, Victoria touched the corner of the paper to the red embers within the open stove. Hollingsworth groaned as the paper ignited, flames consuming it in a moment. Dr. Whitman guided the young woman back to her chair, where she dropped her head into her hands and wept.

"Now, it's your turn, Mr. Hollingsworth." Rose stood before the man and extended the second piece of paper. "Take it."

"No! You can't make me!"

Detective Donahue gave the chair a violent shove. "But I can. Take the paper."

Rose delighted in the response the detective's menacing threat produced in Hollingsworth. He sagged in the chair and accepted the paper. "I can't walk to the stove."

"You don't have to." Rose reached into the stove and pulled out a burning stick and thrust it through the center of the paper Hollingsworth held.

The man screamed and dropped the paper into his lap as

flames licked up the brittle paper. He brushed the blackened paper onto the floor with his one good hand, then spit out a string of profanities that the detective ended with a heavy hand clutched at the back of the man's neck.

"That's enough." The detective's knuckles whitened as he increased the pressure on McAllister's neck.

"And now, Mr. McAllister," Rose said.

Dr. Whitman released the gag covering the man's mouth and gave Rose a most provocative smile. He was enjoying this, too.

"This one is for you." She placed the last paper in his hands.

"Just bring the match here, if you please," the big man said, and there was even a tone of begrudging respect when he made his request.

Rose lit a match.

McAllister's sagging expression resembled her Basset Hound's as he looked to her. "We could have made a fortune."

"At the cost of how many people's lives, Mr. McAllister?"

McAllister touched the corner of the paper to the flame.

CHAPTER 29

Rose held her cup of tea just below her nose and took in a deep breath. Coffee had its place, but nothing was as satisfying as the fragrance of Earl Grey first thing in the morning. Mrs. Pennyworth set a plate before her with a single cherry tart on it. Something in the housekeeper's eye warned Rose not to ask why there was but one.

"I've got the picnic basket packed for you and the doctor," the housekeeper said as she touched a finger to the side of the teapot, as was her custom to test its warmth. "I'll freshen the pot." Mrs. Pennyworth picked up the teapot and started for the kitchen door.

"Mrs. Pennyworth, about last night."

The housekeeper replied in her droll manner, "What about it?"

"I did not know you knew how to handle a firearm. You fired it as though you'd had some experience, and your aim was remarkably precise," Rose said, peering at the woman shimmering on the other side of the steam rising from her teacup.

"Maybe it was. Maybe it wasn't. Maybe I was aiming at his head and I missed. You don't know everything about me, do you, even if you are a lady dee-tec-tive."

"Mrs. Pennyworth, won't you tell me?"

The housekeeper folded her arms high on her chest. She pursed her lips, staring at Rose a moment, then said, "My dad taught me. He had a reputation, you might say—with weapons." The housekeeper thought this was sufficient answer and walked toward the kitchen.

"But the .45? It's not one I'd expect a woman to carry, let alone be able to handle with such ease."

"He favored the Peacemaker most of his life. Gave it to me before he died," Mrs. Pennyworth said with no further elaboration.

There was a finality in the way she delivered this last bit of information, and Rose knew she'd concluded the discussion. But her curiosity was aroused, and one day she'd have to ask. What kind of reputation did Mrs. Pennyworth's father earn and how?

While she was contemplating the occupations for a man with a reputation for using guns, Mrs. Pennyworth returned with a large envelope. "A delivery boy brought this for you. Must be from that Mr. O'Brien, the reporter, judging from the return address stamped in the corner." She swept a small crumb from the tablecloth onto her open palm, disinclined to leave at the moment.

Rose pulled the single typewritten sheet of paper from the envelope. It was the article reporting last night's events, and beneath the proposed headline was the man's byline. Jake O'Brien.

SAMANTHA ST. CLAIRE

Lady Private Eye Breaks Blackmail Case

"Private Eye. What a ridiculous name! Detection solves cases. The brain's ability to sort through the myriad of clues, rejecting those unimportant and focusing on those with significance. Of course, Private Brain would look a little ludicrous in print." She was, more accurately described, a detective. She closed her eyes and took in a deep breath, then opened them to read the rest of the story.

> *Last night brought a dramatic conclusion to the six-year reign of intimidation and violence started by the late Raymond Larson. With a theatrical display of her detective skills, Miss Rose McKenzie identified Raymond Larson as the man behind Denver's rise in crime and the inability of our judicial personages to prosecute known felons in recent years. She discovered the blackmailing file that has crippled our city's judicial system, a file that was destroyed last evening before this reporter's eyes.*

Yes, that should do nicely. It was gratifying to learn that Jake O'Brien wrote with a distinct dramatic flair of his own. He'd make a fine writer of fiction if journalism did not work out for him. With such a gathering of witnesses as the article listed, the

THE CASE OF THE PECULIAR INHERITANCE

search, the break-ins, and assaults should end.

With uncharacteristic attentiveness, Mrs. Pennyworth refilled Rose's teacup, then took a step back to brush more nonexistent crumbs from the table. "Good article?" she asked nonchalantly.

"It will do the job as I intended, yes," Rose said before taking a tentative sip at her cup. "Would you like to read it?"

"Oh, I suppose I could wait until it comes out in the paper this evening."

"All right." Rose folded the paper and was about to return it to the envelope when her housekeeper cleared her throat.

Mrs. Pennyworth wore an expectant expression. "Well, since you'd probably don't have time before Dr. Whitman arrives, I could take a peek and then take it upstairs for you."

From the moment Rose greeted Dr. Whitman and looked into those amber highlights sparkling in his eyes and the ridiculous grin sprawling diagonally across his face, she knew something quite remarkable had occurred to alter his appearance. She imagined that this was how he'd looked as a boy at Christmas, perhaps after receiving his first rocking horse. She'd loathed hers, but the doctor struck her as one child who'd have ridden his in rapturous delight for hours at a time.

"You have a look about you of having grasped the brass ring on the merry-go-round," Rose said as the doctor helped her with her wrap.

He rested his hands on her shoulders and whispered into her

ear, "I want you to close your eyes."

"I'm not fond of surprises," Rose said.

"Yes, well, humor me for once."

Rose stared at him for a long will-testing moment, then begrudgingly acquiesced.

With a firm grip on her elbow, he guided her through the door and out onto the front porch. "All right. You can open your eyes."

Parked at the curb was a gleaming, black, electric locomobile. "Isn't she beautiful? She's called a Victoria," he said.

"I thought you were going to purchase a steam locomobile? I don't think I've seen one like it in town before."

"It's the first one in Denver. One of my patients sold it to me. He's moving to San Francisco and doesn't want to bother with shipping it by train. Said he'll buy another one there." Dr. Whitman ran his hand along the front fender with a gleam of unmistakable delight on his face. "He practically gave it to me."

"Did you save his life, doctor, for him to be so generous?"

"Well, not exactly. He says he's got the speed up to that of a train engine. He actually ran the car beside the track and tested it."

"That sounds thrilling, but I'm still pondering how one cannot exactly save a life."

"It was his daughter," the doctor said somewhat dismissively. He planted his fists on his hips, addressing the machine. "She even looks fast."

"Why is *it* a *she*? What about this machine gives you an impression of femininity?"

Dr. Whitman stuck his thumbs in his vest pockets and turned

the question back to her. "Why did the maker give her the name Victoria?"

"I don't know. I wish you'd explain that to me." Rose contemplated potential explanations, and none of them pleased her. A woman should not be equated to a machine, or rather a person should not equate a machine to a woman. It was degrading. She supposed it was because men perceived both machines and women as servants, doing the master's bidding. She resolved to name her locomobile Winston after her great-aunt's butler.

Dr. Whitman trotted to the passenger door and held it open, reaching for her hand. "Climb in, Miss McKenzie, and we'll see what she can do."

For the better part of the hour, he did exactly that, weaving through the city streets to the fanfare of irate horsemen and wagon drivers. But Victoria's speed dropped appreciably when the asphalt of the city gave way to the unpaved roads leading up into the hills north of Denver. She struggled on the rough terrain, and her springs did little to ease the discomfort of her passengers.

Rose flinched as they approached another length of ruts.

Their conversation had taken a hiatus of necessity as the doctor concentrated on keeping his new locomobile from falling into one of the many cavernous pits. "These roads need improvement." It was an obvious statement, but someone had to say it for the sake of poor Victoria doing her best to prove her worth.

Despite her earlier annoyance with the doctor, Rose felt a pang of sympathy. "You have convinced me, doctor."

"Of what?"

"I will purchase one of my own."

The doctor pulled to the side of the road beneath the glowing leaves of a grove of aspen. "Really?"

"I've learned of an electric locomobile manufactured by a Viennese company. There are some wonderful articles that report they're expecting to create the first electric and gas-powered vehicle in the first years of the next century. Just think, Dr. Whitman, you wouldn't have to limit your touring to the foothills of Denver."

"That's remarkable."

"In fact, I've already invested in the company."

"You're investing?"

"Yes. Why do you look surprised? They are quite reputable. In fact, the royal house has commissioned Mr. Lohner as a coach builder for the Austrian emperor. The man responsible for the engine designs is a man by the name of Porsche, but I think he is of a lesser-known reputation." Rose pulled open the lid of their picnic basket. "You still look surprised."

"You're investing in a locomobile company."

"Yes. That's what I said," she replied placidly.

The doctor sat back against the leather upholstery, which was, Rose had to admit, quite comfortable when they weren't bumping across the rutted roads.

He ran a hand down the side of his face and said, "I forget that about you."

"Forget what?"

"That money is not an issue for you like it is for most of us who are not living on Capitol Hill."

Rose offered the doctor a beef pie along with a napkin. "Once I receive my locomobile, I propose we race to the top of Pikes Peak, you in Victoria and me in Winston."

His perplexed expression relaxed after a few seconds had passed, and he shook his head as a smile lifted the corners of his mouth. "I will race you on one condition, Miss McKenzie."

"What, pray tell, is that?"

The doctor's attractive eyes made that unnerving shift, appearing more lupine than human. He lifted a finger to the tip of her chin and said, "The condition being, that occasionally you allow me to catch you."

Thank you for reading
The Case of the Peculiar Inheritance

Don't miss out on future books from Samantha!
www.samanthastclaire.com/subscribe

Did you know Rose's sister, Cassandra "Casey" McKenzie, has her own book? Don't miss *The Case of the Copper King* by MK McClintock, another stand-alone novel in the McKenzie Sisters Mystery Series.

ABOUT THE AUTHOR

Samantha St. Claire is the pen name of an author passionate about American history and the people whose legacies are woven into the fabric of a nation. She writes these characters to life in her novels of the western frontier, their trials and triumphs. Coming from a family of pioneers, she honestly claims her roots as a Daughter of the American Revolution and descendant of a Scottish Laird.

Never faint of heart, her signature protagonists face the hazards of the frontier with courage, wit, and a healthy pinch of humor.

Sign up for Samantha's newsletter at www.samanthastclaire.com for early notifications of new releases and interesting news relevant to readers of historical fiction.

www.ingramcontent.com/pod-product-compliance
Lightning Source LLC
LaVergne TN
LVHW031615060526
838200LV00007B/217